He studied her a ~~boys to bring the tires.~~

boys to bring the tires.

Brown hair with wisps of gray peeked out from her *kapp*. Hope had a button nose and wide eyes that seemed to take in everything. She directed her boys with kindness and obvious affection.

Within ten minutes, they had the clothesline braced. It might hold until the following Saturday. When Amos explained who he was and why he was there, Hope invited him inside for a cup of tea.

"If it's no trouble..."

"No trouble at all."

He followed her into the house, but there was no table to sit at. Amos doubted there were cups or tea.

She blushed slightly as she turned in a circle, as if hoping something might appear where there was so obviously nothing. "We've just moved in and aren't quite settled yet. I'm not sure what I was thinking. I do have coffee, as Ezekiel brought some over. Or I can offer you a cup of water."

"I'm *gut*, but *danki*." His gaze met hers and enough understanding passed between them that she nodded and dropped the subject of refreshments.

Vannetta Chapman has published over one hundred articles in Christian family magazines and received over two dozen awards from Romance Writers of America chapter groups. She discovered her love for the Amish while researching her grandfather's birthplace of Albion, Pennsylvania. Her first novel, *A Simple Amish Christmas*, quickly became a bestseller. Chapman lives in Texas Hill Country with her husband.

Books by Vannetta Chapman

Love Inspired

Indiana Amish Market

An Amish Proposal for Christmas
Her Amish Adversary
An Unusual Amish Winter Match
The Mysterious Amish Bachelor
A Courtship for the Amish Spinster
An Amish Widow's New Love

Indiana Amish Brides

A Widow's Hope
Amish Christmas Memories
A Perfect Amish Match
The Amish Christmas Matchmaker
An Unlikely Amish Match
The Amish Christmas Secret
An Amish Winter
"Stranded in the Snow"
The Baby Next Door
An Amish Baby for Christmas
The Amish Twins Next Door

Visit the Author Profile page at LoveInspired.com for more titles.

AN AMISH WIDOW'S NEW LOVE

VANNETTA CHAPMAN

LOVE INSPIRED
INSPIRATIONAL ROMANCE

LOVE INSPIRED®
INSPIRATIONAL ROMANCE

ISBN-13: 978-1-335-93712-4

An Amish Widow's New Love

Recycling programs for this product may not exist in your area.

Love Inspired
22 Adelaide St. West, 41st Floor
Toronto, Ontario M5H 4E3, Canada
www.LoveInspired.com

Printed in U.S.A.

There is a friend that sticketh closer than a brother.
—*Proverbs* 18:24

A loving heart is the truest wisdom.
—Charles Dickens

This book is dedicated to Mary Sue Seymour.

Chapter One

April
Shipshewana, Indiana

It was nearly three thirty on a Thursday afternoon when Bus 457 pulled into the small station in Shipshewana. Hope Lambright and her three boys clambered out, gathered their things and proceeded to walk from the bus stop to the little home she'd purchased sight unseen. According to the map the Realtor had sent, the building was only a mere six blocks away, and it wasn't as if they had a lot of luggage. They each carried a suitcase, though when Isaac struggled with his, John reached over and took it in his left hand.

"I can do it," Isaac argued. "But thanks."

"No problem, little *bruder.*"

Which caused Lucas, her middle son, to scowl even more fiercely. "Why did we have to move here, Mamm? This town is so little."

"Smaller than Lancaster, that's for sure and certain." John pointed out the sign for JoJo's Pretzels, Lolly's Fabric Shop and the Blue Gate Restaurant and Theater. "Should be someone willing to give me a job."

The business section didn't last long, and then they were

in a neighborhood of older houses that started out fairly nice but quickly became less cared for and poorer.

Hope stopped on the sidewalk, checking the address on the mailbox and even pulling out the letter from the Realtor to be sure she had the right place.

Yeah.

This was it.

"What is with this house?" For once, Lucas wasn't merely being negative. He was voicing the same question they were all asking themselves.

They'd stopped in front of a small home that looked a bit worse than the picture the Realtor had shown her on the website. Hope braced her shoulders and made a gallant effort to steel her resolve.

"Nothing a little soap and water won't cure." Hope plastered on a smile. She did that a lot these days, in the sincere belief that it would one day feel natural. So far, it hadn't.

"If you say so." Lucas dropped his suitcase onto the rickety porch and stuck his hands in his pockets.

No doubt he was wishing for his phone, but Hope had sat her three boys down and assured them there would be no such foolishness here. This was their fresh start. She had exacted a promise from each of them, before leaving Lancaster, that they wouldn't mess up this second chance with reckless expenditures or impulsive decisions.

She carefully climbed the porch steps that would have to be repaired, put the house key into the lock and jiggled it to no avail.

"Let me try that, Mamm." John took the key from her, brushed it against his pants as if dirt might be the problem and placed it into the lock.

The key had been waiting for them at the bus station, in an envelope with the words *Lambright Family* penned on the outside. Those two words had given Hope a tiny surge of optimism. A feeling that was quickly evaporating as she watched John push his shoulder into the door in order to wrestle it open.

They stepped into a house that was smaller and dingier than the one they'd left. In Lancaster, they'd at least had their things to brighten their small home—things they'd sold to purchase the bus tickets here. Items they'd decided to part with so that they might have their big second chance. The money from the sale of their old home had been barely enough to cover the cost of the new home. It had all been a risky endeavor, but she'd prayed and worried and hoped and prayed some more. In the end, given Lucas's propensity to find trouble, she'd decided to take the big step of moving her family.

As she stood just inside the front door allowing regret to overtake her earlier optimism, her three boys walked through the house.

"It'll be okay," John assured her as he returned to the living room. "We'll get some paint."

"Yes, we will." She smiled at her oldest, reached up and patted his face. He ducked away, which helped her mood to rebound. John had lately decided that at seventeen he was too old for open displays of affection. He always smiled at her mischievously as he sidestepped her hugs. The important thing was that her oldest took things seriously, took life seriously. He had always been an encouragement to her.

Lucas walked back into the living room. "Only two bedrooms? Tell me I don't have to share with Isaac and John."

"Unless one of us gets married—*ya*, you do." John laughed. "Let's see what Isaac has found in the backyard."

Hope walked through the two bedrooms separated by one small bath. The wood floors would clean up. They might even shine with enough elbow grease. The walls would have to be painted though. Not only were they a terrible color somewhere between off-white and taupe, they were also dirty. Only two pieces of furniture had been left—two beds in the boys' room. The frames were intact, though there were no headboards. There also were no mattresses, but each bed had a decrepit box spring. Why had someone taken the mattresses but left the box springs?

The beds looked like they needed to be taken out to the curb and left for the garbage truck.

They'd start hitting garage sales the next day. Though without a horse and buggy to use for bringing items home, relocating anything they purchased would be a problem.

The old familiar weight threatened to settle on her. Before it had a chance, she walked into the kitchen then smiled. Sunlight poured through the back windows and turned the small kitchen and dining area into a haven of light. The bank of windows that stretched across the entire room went a long way toward raising her spirits. They were dirt-smudged like everything else in the house, but dirt could be wiped away.

Hope walked to the refrigerator, opened it out of habit and was surprised to see a box of fried chicken, containers of potato salad and beans, a six-pack of soda, a carton of milk and a box of cinnamon rolls. A note pinned to the box of fried chicken said, "Welcome to your new home! Your first meal is on us." It was signed by Babs Jones, the Realtor that Hope had worked with throughout the last six weeks.

Hope could put off her trip to the grocer until the next day. They had dinner and breakfast. John and Lucas had beds to sleep on, though there were no sheets. They'd each packed one blanket that could be laid over the box springs. Isaac was still young enough to think of it as an adventure to sleep on the floor, and Hope didn't mind doing so either. The important thing was that they had a roof over their heads.

She was grateful for those simple things. Moving closer to the window, she stood there studying her boys in the afternoon light. The backyard had an old chain-link fence around it that was sagging in places. A swing hung from a maple tree. Isaac laughed as he pumped his legs—going higher and higher. Lucas had plopped onto the ground and was lying on his back staring up at the clear blue Indiana sky. John was walking the perimeter, checking things out.

Next to the house was a small lot with a newish barn and enough pasture for a single horse—maybe two. The Realtor had assured Hope that the owner would be happy to rent it out to them once they had a horse and buggy.

Paint.

Furniture.

Bedding.

Dishes.

Food.

A horse and buggy.

She stopped her thoughts before the growing list overwhelmed her. She stopped her thoughts before they returned to the latest letter from Edwin Bing that was sitting in her purse unopened. She knew what it said. She didn't know how to fix that situation. She wanted to do the right thing, but in that particular case she didn't know how. So, she pushed the worry to the back of her mind. There was enough in front of her to attend to without focusing on what waited for them back in Lancaster.

Back in Lancaster.

Nein. She wouldn't dwell on that.

They would make this new life in Shipshewana work. God hadn't abandoned them. Yes, she'd made poor decisions in her life. Yes, the boys' father had been unreliable at best and irresponsible at his worst—but he had loved them in his own way. His death two years earlier had been a blow.

Now they were starting over.

This was their grand second chance.

And she wasn't about to see it go to waste.

As had become his custom on Saturday mornings, Amos Yoder met his bishop at the Cozy Corner Café for breakfast. It wasn't as if he had children at home that needed him there. His five girls were all married and busy with families of their own. The breakfast with Ezekiel had probably started out of pity for Amos as his family shrank, but as with most things it had quickly turned into a habit they both looked forward to.

They'd been through a lot together. Ezekiel had performed Amos's marriage to Lydia all those years ago. He'd been present for all five of his girls' births, for his wife's passing, for his girls' baptisms and weddings, and even for the birth of his grandchildren. Ezekiel was more than his bishop. He was as close as a *bruder*.

After greeting his friend and nodding to the waitress, indicating that he'd love a cup of coffee, he asked, "Why the frown on this beautiful April day?"

"We have a new family in town." Ezekiel paused, as if he were considering his words. "A new Amish family, and I believe they need our help."

"Tell me more."

"After we order," Ezekiel said. "I see you eyeing the plate of biscuits and gravy our waitress was carrying."

Amos had a fondness for any type of fresh bread, as well as most foods that were sweet or salty. His *doschdern* made sure there were few such things in his kitchen—fortunately, their influence hadn't yet reached to the Cozy Corner Café.

Once they'd ordered, Ezekiel picked up the conversation where they'd left it. "Hope Lambright is forty-six years old. She is a widow with three sons. John is seventeen, Lucas is fifteen and the youngest lad—Isaac—is ten. They arrived two days ago, moved here from Lancaster, looking for a new start."

Those last five words hung between them for a moment. Amos understood there were many reasons families started over. He didn't need to know the particulars about the Lambright family, and Ezekiel would only share what was necessary. So instead of probing for details, Amos asked, "How can I help?"

Their conversation was again interrupted as Jenny placed two platters of the day's special in front of them, complete with biscuits and gravy. They silently blessed the food, as was their custom, and dug in.

When Ezekiel had pushed his plate away and Amos had his coffee cup refilled, they picked up the topic once more.

"I've secured employment for John with Stephen Miller."

"Helping with the buggy tours?"

"Yup. The Lambrights have no buggy or horse, so transportation is a bit of a challenge."

"Stephen can swing by and pick the boy up."

"Exactly."

"Smart thinking. Let me guess. You're still looking for employment for Lucas, the fifteen-year-old."

"I am."

It wasn't unusual for Ezekiel to let Amos know about such needs. As the largest employer of Amish in town, he often had a spot open…or he could make a spot. The Shipshewana Outdoor Market was the largest of its kind in the Midwest and was growing in crowd size and number of employees every year. As owner, Amos was still in charge of hiring, though he'd officially turned over the general manager position to his son-in-law Gideon.

"I'd be happy to hire the boy," Amos said. "But what aren't you saying? That glint in your eye tells me there's more."

"Indeed. Hope shared with me that Lucas has been a bit of a challenge. I won't go into the details. Those are hers to share with you should she feel the need, but the boy may require a kind but firm guiding hand."

"Okay." Amos would have liked additional specifics about a perspective employee, but apparently Ezekiel had said all he planned to on the subject.

The bishop grinned, pulled a small sheet of paper from his pocket and slid it across the table. "That's Hope's address. It would be good if you could stop by today."

Amos frowned at the address. He knew it well enough. One of the poorer rentals in their small town that had gone up for sale a month or so ago. He'd been surprised when he'd learned that someone had bought the place. If he remembered correctly, the house looked as if it would fall over in a good wind.

"I assume we'll be having a workday there soon."

"Next Saturday. The family came into town Thursday afternoon with the clothes on their backs and nothing more. We'll be coordinating donations as well as painting and shoring up the place on the workday. Until then, I dropped off a few bags of groceries and some bedding."

"Sounds *gut*."

Ezekiel stood, so Amos did, too.

"Let me walk you out," Amos said, slipping a ten-dollar tip onto the table.

The April sunshine felt good on his face. Amos was self-aware enough to realize he'd been out of sorts since his youngest *doschder*, Eunice, had married the previous month.

He had worried about his girls for so long that it was possible he had forgotten how to pay attention to his own needs. At sixty years old, he'd made the decision to retire in three months, but then what would he do? He preferred working, even if it wasn't necessary financially.

Still, it was their way to hand the reins over to sons. Though Amos had all daughters, his sons-in-law were good men and hard workers. Gideon would take over the market. He'd do an excellent job.

After walking Ezekiel to the parking area where their horse and buggies waited, Amos decided he might as well visit the Lambright family before running his Saturday errands. He climbed into his buggy and called out to Peanut. The mare was cream colored and young enough still to enjoy the outing. She set off down the road at a nice trot. The drive from the café to the Lambright home was less than a mile and wound through several blocks of homes.

On arriving, he directed Peanut over to the curb, hoping he'd remembered the wrong address but knowing he hadn't. This was it, all right. The home was worse than he'd remembered. The structure looked rotted in some places, was sorely in need of paint and no doubt had a roof that leaked. It was also small for four people. He guessed it topped out at eight hundred square feet. Two bedrooms and one bath, a tiny kitchen and living room. It could have been a nice starter home for a newly married couple—if it were renovated. As a home for a mom and three growing boys, it would be a challenge.

He walked up the porch steps carefully, as the boards were rotted in places. A young boy answered his knock on the door.

"You must be Isaac."

"Yes."

"My name is Amos. Is your mother home?"

"Yes." The boy offered a rueful smile and tugged on his right earlobe. "She's hanging clothes on the line. Want me to get her?"

"How about we walk around back together?"

"Okay."

Isaac jogged down the steps and led Amos around the house and through a rickety gate. A woman wearing traditional Amish clothing was attempting to hang pants on a clothesline. The problem was that the poles of the clothesline were tilting inward, so the line itself curved downward. An older boy lay in the grass, tossing an old baseball into the air and catching it.

"Mamm, we have company," Isaac said.

She turned in surprise, lost her grip on the clothesline, and the entire thing sagged to the ground.

"Let me help you with that." Amos walked to the far pole, pulled it into an upright position, then looked around for a way to brace it there. Ezekiel would need to add *new clothesline* to his list of workday projects. "Perhaps your son could bring some of those old tires over."

"*Gut* idea. Isaac, run and get one of those tires. Be sure there are no snakes or water in it."

When she turned back to Amos, he inclined his head toward the older boy, who was still tossing the baseball.

"Lucas, go and help your brother."

"We'll need several," Amos added.

The boy started to argue. With his mother or with Amos? Remaining silent, he reined in his response, slowly stood and trudged to the back of the yard.

"Boys will be boys." Hope tried to put some good-natured teasing into her voice, but it fell flat.

How had she even washed the laundry? In the sink?

Amos's *doschder* Bethany and her husband, Aaron, had recently purchased a gently used newer machine. Amos made a mental note to see about bringing the older one to Hope.

He studied her as they waited for the boys to bring the tires. Brown hair with wisps of gray peeked out from her *kapp*. She had a button nose and wide eyes that seemed to take in everything. She was shorter than Amos's five foot ten and a half inches, and she was wispy thin. She directed her boys with kindness and obvious affection.

Within ten minutes, they had the clothesline braced. It might hold until the following Saturday. When Amos explained who he was and why he was there, Hope invited him inside for a cup of tea.

"If it's no trouble."

"No trouble at all."

He followed her into the house, but there was no table to sit at. Amos doubted there were cups or tea.

She blushed slightly as she turned in a circle, as if hoping something might appear where there was nothing. "We've just moved in and aren't quite settled yet. I'm not sure what I was thinking. I do have coffee, as Ezekiel brought some over. Or I can offer you a cup of water."

"I'm *gut*, but *danki*." His gaze met hers and enough understanding passed between them that she nodded and dropped the subject of refreshments.

There wasn't any furniture in the dining nook or the living room.

"How about we sit on the front porch?" Amos suggested. "I wanted to talk to you about hiring your middle son…if he's looking for a job, that is."

"Oh, he's looking. Rather, he's supposed to be looking."

Together, they walked through the empty living area and out the front door. There were no chairs on the porch, but

Amos sat with his back against a center post. Hope sat with her legs swinging over the edge of the porch. It was a position that made her look much younger than her forty-six years, though the worry lines etched on her face confirmed that any youth she possessed had fled long ago. Still, there was something striking about her.

"Ezekiel spoke with you?" She didn't look away when she asked the question.

"Yes."

"But we just arrived on Thursday. He only came to see us yesterday."

Amos shrugged.

"He told you that Lucas needed a job?"

"He did. I run the outdoor market, so I'm always on the lookout for good employees."

"I can only hope Lucas will be that."

"Do you have reservations?"

"Oh, yes, Mr. Yoder."

"Please, call me Amos."

"Yes, Amos. I have reservations regarding my middle son." She sat tall and again looked directly at him.

"We've had a few difficult years. Actually, that's not the truth. All of our years, since my oldest was born, have been difficult. When my husband passed, Lucas took it the hardest. There was…" She exhaled then gathered her courage. "There was trouble in Lancaster. Lucas took to the wrong crowd, lost not one but two jobs, and seemed adrift. He still seems that way."

"I understand."

She cocked her head. "I think you do, and I appreciate that you're offering him a chance to prove himself."

"If you're willing to let him work at the market, I'm willing to take him on. The position would be temporary, and he'd receive a review in ninety days. At that point, we'd visit the subject of permanent employment."

"That sounds quite fair."

"Perhaps we should include Lucas in this discussion."

"Of course." She stood. "I'll fetch him."

The boy followed his mother back around to the front porch, looking as if he were being pulled in her wake somewhat against his will.

"Lucas, my name is Amos Yoder. I'm the owner of the outdoor market here in town. Our bishop, Ezekiel, told me you were looking for employment. Do you have any experience working with tourists?"

"Nein. I had a few part-time jobs over the years, but nothing like that.*"*

"Would you be interested in gaining experience?"

A shrug.

They spoke for another few minutes about what his job would entail. Hope asked a few questions. Lucas rarely made eye contact and when he did, it was to glare at whomever he was addressing. He stood with his shoulders slumped, his hair obscuring his vision and his hands tucked into his pockets. His answers were limited to grunts and short declarative sentences.

Finally, Amos asked, "How do you feel about working six hours a day?"

"Guess I don't have much choice." This time, the glare was directed toward his mother.

"Lucas, Amos is offering you a *wunderbaar* opportunity. It would be appropriate for you to thank him."

"Danki," he mumbled in the direction of the ground.

It was settled that Lucas would begin at the market on Tuesday, would walk to work, and his shift would start at 9:00 a.m. sharp. The only sign of interest from the boy came when Amos told him the hourly rate he'd be making. It wasn't great, but it wasn't the lowest in town either. Amos believed in compensating his employees as well as he could.

"You'll work from nine until three thirty, with a thirty-minute break for lunch, and you can eat for free at the canteen."

"Okay."

"Do you have any questions about what you'll be doing?"

"I guess not."

"All right then. I look forward to seeing you in my office first thing Tuesday morning."

The boy muttered something, realized he was dismissed and ambled off, shoulders hunched, head down, hands in his pockets.

Hope's youngest son, Isaac, had found his way to the front yard by the time the impromptu interview was ending. "I could work at the market," he declared. "I'm stronger than I look, and I take instructions real good."

The boy grinned impishly at Amos and then his *mamm.* Amos felt a tug on his heart. Isaac reminded him of his own *grandkinner.*

"Come and see me when you're…" Amos held his hand at the five-foot mark. "About this tall."

"That may be a while." Isaac frowned. "Plus, Mamm says I can't work because I have to go to school. I just wish I could earn some money, too—like John and Lucas."

"School is important." Amos liked Isaac's attitude, so he added, "I imagine your *mamm* will need your help around here once school lets out."

Isaac brightened. "I am a great helper."

"You are indeed," Hope said. "You could start by picking up any sticks in the backyard. We want it clean so you and your *bruders* can play ball back there."

"I'm on it!" He turned, took three steps, turned back and walked up to Amos, his open palm held high.

Amos slapped the boy's palm, feeling somewhat silly. Isaac smiled broadly, slapped his *mamm*'s hand, then took off at a trot to the backyard.

"Isaac. Means laughter, *ya*?" The twinkle in Hope's eyes banished some of the tiredness and defeat.

She looked younger. She looked beautiful.

Amos jerked his thoughts away from that path. He was much too old to be thinking about a woman's attractiveness. He searched his mind for something—anything—else to say. "Ezekiel told me your oldest is working for Stephen Miller."

"Yes. He started today."

"Stephen's a *gut* man, and a *gut* boss."

"So Ezekiel said." She paused, looking embarrassed. "What would really help is if I could find a job."

"You?" He couldn't quite keep the surprise from his voice.

"I can't let my boys carry the responsibility of this household on their young shoulders. I don't suppose you have anything at the market for someone my age?"

"Umm. Well, what is your work history?"

"I've held a few part-time jobs over the years, but for the most part I've focused on being a *mamm*."

"Right. Of course."

"I learn quickly though, and I work hard." The look she gave him was so vulnerable that Amos had to look away.

"I don't... That is to say, I'm not certain..." He thought of the unmanned desk outside his office. But he didn't need a secretary. Did he? Given his impending retirement, he only had three months left at the market himself.

As if she could read his mind, Hope added, "Even something temporary would be helpful. I could get some experience, and perhaps then someone would be willing to hire me permanently."

He couldn't do it. He couldn't deny this woman a second chance. "All right. Come and see me first thing Tuesday morning."

"At the market?"

"Yes. Come to the office, and we'll see what we can find for you."

"*Danki*, Mr. Yoder."

"Amos."

"Danki, Amos." She rubbed a hand around the back of her neck, massaging at the muscles there. "I'll make arrangements for Isaac to be picked up from school. Maybe it would be okay for him to stay here alone for just a few hours. He is ten, after all."

"Not necessary. We have childcare for our employees. Several of the *youngies* are assigned to watch workers' children. They even take a horse and buggy to the school to pick them up. If you're comfortable with that."

"Yes. That would be *wunderbaar*."

Amos hopped down off the porch and straightened his straw hat. "Excellent. I suppose I'll see you Tuesday then."

"Nine a.m. sharp. Same as Lucas."

"Sounds perfect." Amos had always arrived early so that he could get a jump on the day's work. He'd definitely need to be there early on Tuesday. What kind of state had he left his office in? And what of the secretarial space? He seemed to remember some towering stacks of paper.

"You're not having second thoughts, are you?"

"Not at all." He wished her a good day and walked away from the sad little house on Walnut Lane.

Lucas would be a challenge, and hadn't he been looking for just that? Not that he knew a thing about raising boys.

He'd had five girls. Five girls between the ages of one and eleven when his wife had passed. He could certainly sympathize with the difficulties that Hope was experiencing.

The question was how much he could help.

And whether he was willing to get emotionally involved.

Donating money or bedding or clothing was easy enough and everyone in their community would do those things. Attempting to mentor her angry son would require an emotional involvement that he wasn't sure he was ready for. Having Hope work as his secretary would require that he see and interact with her every day. He had his own routines, his own ways of doing things, though if he were honest with himself, the filing and phone answering were both growing old. Plus he was set to retire on July 1.

Had he really just offered a temporary job to Hope Lambright? He had. Indeed, he had. He drove the buggy home, barely noticing the fine spring day. Instead, he stewed over what he'd managed to get himself into. It had only been a few hours ago that he'd left his home thinking there was little new to experience, little to separate one day from another.

More than one person he'd spoken to about it had assured him that retirement was something one grew used to. The golden years. A hard-earned reward. The third act of his life.

Did he want that? He wasn't sure.

Did he want to get involved with a new and needy family? He wasn't sure about that either.

He had asked the Lord for a new challenge even as he'd driven toward the diner and Ezekiel and ultimately Hope. The entire situation reminded him of something his own *mamm* had been fond of saying. *Be careful what you ask for.*

Chapter Two

Amos had a chance to share a private conversation with his son-in-law Gideon after their Sunday luncheon. It was an off Sunday, so there was no church service. They occasionally invited other families to eat with them, but today it was just Amos, his five daughters, their husbands and his seven grandchildren.

He couldn't help thinking of Hope and her sons. In fact, he'd thought of her quite often since meeting her the day before. Why was that? Because their situations were so similar? Because he was second-guessing his commitment? Because he was lonely?

He wondered if she would be feeling homesick.

Or lonesome.

Or afraid.

Ezekiel would have invited her to dinner and no doubt gone and picked them up. He was that kind of bishop.

"Whatcha looking so studious about, Amos?" Gideon sat beside him on the front porch swing that overlooked the yard. Becca and Bethany were sitting on an old quilt under a maple tree, surrounded by sleeping babies—their own as well as their nephews and nieces. Sarah and Eunice and Ada had taken the older children to the back pond.

"We're butterfly watching," John had explained as he trotted off with a homemade butterfly net. He ran to catch up with Mary and Lydia, who were each carrying similar nets. Josh was Eunice's stepson and relatively new to the family, but the three children had quickly become the best of friends.

"Amos?" Gideon was looking at him with concern.

"Right. *Ya.* My mind was following the *kinder.* And before that I was mulling over a…situation."

"I'm all ears," Gideon said. "Unless you don't want to talk about it."

"*Nein.* I want… I need to talk about it." Amos had learned long ago that keeping worries to himself only made them seem larger. He explained the situation as succinctly as possible—Hope and the three children, their second chance, the status of the house, the problems with the middle son.

Gideon let out a whistle. "That's a lot."

"Indeed."

"Are you worried about the boy?"

"Yes. I'm not sure he's turned over a new leaf, though it's obvious his *mamm* hopes that he has."

"I'll meet with him Tuesday morning, see what he enjoys doing and try to assign him to a job that he'll be comfortable with."

"You'll be lucky to get a dozen words out of him."

Gideon laughed. "He won't be the first sullen teenager I've worked with. We'll find a place for him."

"*Danki.*"

"*Gem gschehne.*"

The old words should have comforted him. They did comfort him, but Amos still felt oddly off-kilter.

"You're worried about Hope." Gideon studied his father-in-law, a smile stretching across his face. "I suppose you were hoping to sneak off into your retirement without training a new secretary."

"It's not something I've done before. I inherited Miranda King. She trained me more than the other way around." Amos laughed, feeling better just talking about his retired secretary. Miranda had kept their office in tip-top shape for more than twenty years. Twenty years. Sometimes it was difficult for him to accept how much time had passed.

Miranda was solid ground. Hope Lambright was not.

"Is there something more?"

"Like what?"

"Are you…" Gideon drug the word out, then finally caved and finished his own sentence. "Are you interested in Hope?"

"Interested?"

"Romantically speaking."

Amos stood and paced back and forth on the porch. "Of course not. That's ridiculous. I'm sixty years old."

"And yet you're not in the grave yet."

"She has three children, Gideon." He'd been studying the fields, but now he turned and faced his son-in-law. "She has a boy who is only ten. My oldest grandson is nearly that age."

"Josh is only six and he's your step-grandson."

"He's family. And this is all beside the point. In answer to your question—no. I am not romantically interested."

Gideon held up his hands in mock surrender, but muttered, "Me thinks thou protests too much."

Amos chose to ignore that remark. Sitting back down on the swing, he said, "What if it doesn't work out? I don't want to see a single mom unemployed because she can't figure out the intricacies of filing or office management."

"First of all, I doubt that will happen."

"Why?"

"Because any woman who can raise three boys on her own, purchase a home and move those three boys from Pennsylvania to Indiana can certainly file and answer phones."

"I suppose."

"Secondly, even if it did happen, we'll deal with it then."

"How?"

"We'll move her to another spot—maybe in the canteen or working with vendors or helping with the children touring the Backyard Barnyard."

"Okay." Amos blew out a breath. "Okay. You're right. We were looking to add more positions for the upcoming season anyway."

"We sure were."

"And I only promised a temporary position, so she could work through the summer and then find something more appropriate." Which was immediately followed by the thought that maybe by the time they were closed for the fall, she'd have met someone and remarried. That thought should have made him happier, less stressed. Such marriages often did happen quickly when two families were combining based more on need than some youthful idea about love. Did they have any eligible bachelors in their church group?

"Seriously, don't worry about it, Amos. The market is growing. I'm projecting we'll need at least a dozen additional full-time people and maybe another dozen part-time." Gideon put his hands behind his head and stretched his back. "Business is *gut*."

"We have much to be grateful for," Amos agreed.

Gideon patted his shoulder, then stood and walked down the porch steps to join his wife, who was now lying on the blanket, squealing as Baby Abram smothered her with kisses. Reaching the bottom step, he turned back and waited until Amos met his gaze. "It would be okay though, Amos. If you did have romantic feelings."

"I barely know the woman."

"True, but sometimes the heart recognizes these things before the mind. Sometimes you just know."

Those words continued to come back to Amos through the afternoon and all of the next day. *Sometimes you just know.* Nope. That wasn't it at all. He didn't want to disappoint Hope. He wanted her family to settle into a comfortable life here in Shipshewana. Nothing more or less. Or so he told himself, as he continued to make notes on a sheet of paper—things he would need to teach her so that she could help him efficiently run the office.

One thing was certain: it was going to be an interesting week. As he prepared for bed that evening, he picked up the Bible from his nightstand. Running his fingers over the cover, he allowed his mind to drift back. The Bible had been a gift from his parents when he and Lydia had first married. Unlike the new Bibles the *youngies* often owned—Bibles that had the traditional German text on one side and *Englisch* on the other—this Bible was written only in German. He liked reading the scripture in the old language. He enjoyed remembering his parents and grandparents quoting from its pages.

It had all been so long ago.

Forty-two years since he and Lydia had wed.

Nearly twenty-three years since she'd passed.

Their youngest, Ada, had been only a year old. Sarah had been barely eleven at the time. She had become like a mother to Becca, Eunice, Bethany and Ada.

Twenty-three years.

He'd felt lonely often enough since then. But he'd always pushed those feelings away. He had a market to run and a family to raise. Now his *doschdern* had their own families. The market soon would be running without him.

A part of his mind realized that the loneliness he had for

so long kept at bay was pushing in, surrounding him, threatening to swallow him whole. Another part of his mind didn't want to accept that idea. It made him feel older and vulnerable. It made him feel incredibly uncomfortable.

He closed his eyes, prayed for peace, then opened the old text and began to read.

Hope couldn't have explained why she was so nervous. She burned the oatmeal, spilled a cup of coffee and tried to put her left shoe on her right foot.

She'd worked outside the home before. It had been the only way they'd been able to eat some years. Never full-time, but she was acquainted with the stress of getting three children off to school and herself to work.

This was different.

John was already in the kitchen when she walked in, pinning her *kapp* to her head.

"I'm surprised to see you up at this hour," she said.

"I like to get there early." He shrugged his shoulders, which had broadened in the last year, reminding Hope that he was more man than boy.

"And?" She waited, pretty sure she knew what was coming.

"And if I leave early, then Stephen doesn't feel like he has to pick me up."

He kissed her cheek before she could argue, swiped an apple from the bowl of fruit on the table and whistled as he walked out of the house. That kiss reminded her that he was still a boy. If she attempted to show any affection, he ducked away. But a man leaving for work and kissing his *mamm* goodbye? That was perfectly reasonable.

Hope looked around the kitchen. The fruit, the bowl the fruit was in, the coffee, the coffeemaker, even the oatmeal had been given to them. Rachel Beiler had dropped those things and more off a few hours after Ezekiel's visit. The word was out that Hope's family was in need, and the community was responding generously and kindly.

She swallowed any embarrassment she might have felt and poured herself a cup of coffee. She'd long ago made it a habit to give herself thirty minutes alone before the boys needed to be up and about. The coffee and the solitude helped to calm her. This morning she found her mind returning to Amos once more.

Someone had mentioned at Ezekiel's Sunday luncheon that Amos had recently turned sixty. He didn't look sixty. Yes, his brown hair, which curled at the back of his neck, was speckled with gray. But he moved with the agility and energy of a younger man. It was his eyes she kept thinking of—a warm blue with laugh lines fanning out from the corners. It was more than the way he looked that caught her attention though. Amos Yoder took in everything around him—assessing and waiting and then responding. She was suspected he had grasped much more than she had said.

Or perhaps that was the tiredness and stress of the move muddling her thoughts. Who didn't want to be understood? She did, but she'd long ago stopped trying to explain how she'd come to be in this situation. Most people didn't want details. They were befuddled, unable to imagine so many bad turns in one life. She hadn't felt judgement in Amos's gaze though. She'd felt understanding.

Of course, he didn't know how bad her financial situation was. He certainly didn't know about the letters from Edwin Bing. Four in all—every one more outraged and demanding than the last. Why had she kept them all? And what would she do if he learned of her new address? What should she do? Perhaps she should speak to Ezekiel about it.

She stood, rinsed her cup and called her two younger sons to breakfast. An hour later, the three of them made their way to the neighborhood school. There was a larger *Englisch* school several blocks over. The school Isaac would attend was a traditional one-room schoolhouse with a nice outdoor area for the children to play—complete with swings, see-saws, and a baseball diamond.

Isaac was fairly bouncing as they walked, going over everything that had happened the day before even though he'd already told her.

"We have a pet rabbit. Did I tell you about Hoppy? And one student gets to take him home each weekend. Oh, boy. I hope I get to before school's out. There's only a few weeks left. Do you think the teacher will pick me?"

"Tell her you'd like to help, and that we'd be happy to have Hoppy in our home."

"Stupid name," Lucas muttered.

"Is not."

"Is too."

"That's enough."

They stopped outside the school. Though they were a little early, the teacher was already there, as well as a few other students.

Hope straightened Isaac's suspenders, then patted down his cowlick, which immediately popped back up.

"*Mamm.*" He ducked away, then threw his arms around her waist, giving her a much-needed hug.

"Someone will pick you up when school's out," she reminded him.

"How will I know who to go with?"

"They'll find you."

Hope didn't know how to assure him that all would be fine. She didn't know that it would be, but she trusted that the day at school and the afternoon at the market would go well. Amos seemed like a kind man. He'd hired Lucas and herself and offered childcare. He seemed responsible and efficient.

"Have a *wunderbaar* day," she called after her youngest.

Isaac waved, then dashed off into the school. Hope had spoken with the teacher the day before. The woman had seemed capable as well as nice, something that wasn't true of every teacher who had taught her sons.

Hope and Lucas continued toward the market.

"It's stupid we have to come this way. It makes our walk even farther."

"It does, but just think…it also gives us more time to spend together."

Lucas rolled his eyes, but his expression softened a little. "What if I hate this job, Mamm? And why do I have to work? I'm only fifteen."

"Most Amish *youngies* begin working once they're out of school."

"Why?" He seemed genuinely puzzled. "I mean I know why I'm working. I understand we need the money, but why do the wealthier kids work?"

An outsider might assume that everyone in an Amish community was at the same income level. That, of course, was not the truth. Some families were wealthier. Others were poorer. Unlike the *Englisch*, the wealthier Amish didn't buy fancy cars or carry the latest cell phones. But their buggies were a bit nicer. Their clothes fit well. She suspected Amos's family was like that, and she didn't judge him for it. Did she wish the same for her children? Yes, of course she did. Their economic position was something that she'd accepted but never stopped working against.

"God has work for all his children, regardless of age or ability."

"Bible?"

"Amish proverb."

"Doesn't answer my question though." Lucas scowled.

Hope thought that she could watch her middle son scamper down into a dark hidey-hole. His thoughts seemed to lead there naturally. He didn't have the industrious spirit of her oldest or the energetic presence of her youngest.

"Ideally, you would work an apprenticeship—if you knew what you wanted to do. The years from fifteen to eighteen, even fifteen to twenty, are—"

"*Rumspringa. Ya.* I know. Though when I do anything outside the lines, I end up in trouble."

"We can talk about your running around time later tonight if you like, but, Lucas..." Hope stopped on the sidewalk and waited for her son to do the same.

He finally turned and looked at her.

"Perhaps, at the market, you will find the thing that you enjoy doing. If that happens, we'll ask Amos to let you apprentice in that particular area. Until then, do the work they give you and do it well."

Lucas nodded and for once didn't add a negative remark.

Which Hope was going to take as a win.

The market was bigger than she'd imagined. It stretched for acres. The parking area, especially, was huge. Did that many people really visit on the days they were open?

It was easy enough to follow the signs to the office, and Hope was pleased to see they'd arrived a good thirty minutes early. She was wondering whether to go inside or not when the door opened and a man stepped out. He was tallish with blond hair, a muscular build and blue eyes that took them in. A smile spread across his face.

"You must be Hope. I'm Gideon, the general manager here at the market." He lowered his voice and wiggled his eyebrows. "And Amos's son-in-law, which had nothing to do with his hiring me. In fact, I hadn't even met Becca when I first started work here."

"*Gut* to meet you."

"And you must be Lucas."

"*Ya.*"

"Great. You're with me." He gave Hope directions to Amos's office, then he nodded at the boy, who hurried to keep up with his long strides.

Hope whispered a prayer for her son. Standing there in the April sunshine, on the brink of a new adventure, she prayed that Lucas would find some peace and contentment—and direction. "Please, Lord. Show him the way." Finally, she opened her eyes, took in the beautiful spring day, turned and walked into the building where she would step into her new job. She followed signs around to the main office area.

The building itself looked old, but it had been kept up well. The guest area and halls had a beautiful pine floor. What looked like new carpet, fresh paint and tasteful wall art decorated the offices she passed. There were comfortable chairs and big windows with sparkling panes to let in the light.

She followed yet another sign to the main office, came around a corner and stopped abruptly.

"Oh, my." Her fingertips flew to her lips. She stood there gawking because she couldn't quite believe the unleashed chaos in front of her. Was this her job? Amos hadn't said. Only that he would try to find her some work. Well, what she was looking at certainly qualified.

She moved closer and gaped at her desk, or what she supposed was her desk, and almost let out a laugh. Stacks of crisscrossed paper that reminded her of a big game of Jenga covered every available surface. They were towering so high that even the slightest brush against one of the stacks would send papers careening to the floor.

If she was expected to answer the telephone, she'd have to find it first. How many weeks had it been since the filing had been done? Several dead plants adorned the shelves. Stepping closer, she spied enough dust that Isaac could have drawn a picture there. Boxes were stacked against the wall. Some had been opened, but others remained taped shut. A large wicker basket overflowed with unopened mail.

She wasn't sure how long she'd been standing there, staring at the clutter, when she became aware that someone was watching her. She spun around and came face-to-face with her boss. Same kind eyes. Same thoughtful gaze.

"This outer area is quite a mess. I know." Amos tossed her an apologetic smile. "Come into my office. We can talk there."

Hope expected to see the same level of disarray, but Amos's office was in tip-top shape. No papers on the desk. No files stacked on the floor. No dust. There was a story here, and she was probably about to hear it.

She perched on the chair he motioned to.

Amos sat behind the desk, adjusting the reading glasses that sat next to a tablet and pen. He looked so natural there that she almost laughed again. What would that feel like? To work in a job so long that you became a part of that place?

"I've worked at the market all of my adult life. I started as a young man, working at various jobs, and stayed so long they kept promoting me."

"I suspect you were a *gut* worker."

"I was, and I had a family to support—five girls, so I was highly motivated. Worked my way up to general manager and owner."

"Wow."

"*Gotte* is *gut*," he said.

And she automatically replied with, "All the time."

"For most of those years, Miranda King was my secretary. She's the one—" he waved a hand at his clean desk "—who impressed upon me the importance of keeping a neat area. She trained me well. Then, she retired."

"How long ago?" The question popped out before Hope considered how rude it might sound.

If Amos was offended, he didn't show it. In fact, he grinned. "I should have warned you that things were in a state of rather advanced disarray."

"So, that—" She jerked a thumb toward the outer office. "Would be my job?"

"*Ya*, it would. Answer the phone. Take care of the filing. Open the mail. Gideon and I thumbed through it a couple of times each week. We removed anything that seemed to require a timely answer. Same with the boxes and other deliveries." He paused, gazing at the ceiling, as if he were trying to find her other duties written there.

"Remove the dead plants," she suggested. "Dust the shelves. Clean things up a bit."

Lowering his voice, Amos admitted, "It's worse than I realized. I suppose I'd been ignoring it."

"Why did you wait so long to hire someone? I assume Miranda King didn't leave it that way."

Amos paused. He seemed to be considering how much he should say. Finally, he sat back, resting his hands on the desk, his fingers interlaced. "I'm retiring."

"What? When?"

"July 1. That's the plan anyway. Gideon has already taken over as general manager. You met him?"

She nodded. "Seems like a nice young man."

"Good business sense. Hard worker. Great son-in-law."

Amos looked uncomfortable. "I suppose I thought it would be best to let Gideon hire his own secretary."

"But then I asked for a job."

"You did, and I do need someone."

Something in her heart sank. She'd been telling herself that if she did well, if she proved herself, that this job might turn into something permanent. She'd been telling herself that she could begin sending money to Edwin Bing and that particular problem would go away. But she couldn't pay off three thousand dollars of debt with a temporary job.

Why was it that they could never happen upon a permanent solution to their problems? Still, work was work. And the money would help to pay their bills for as long as she could keep the job.

"So, this is temporary."

"It is." He again hesitated, seemed about to say something, then shook his head. "I'm sorry."

"No need to apologize." She gave him what she hoped was a sparkling smile. It felt rather tight and artificial, but at the moment it was the best she could do. "I'm sure it will be valuable experience for me."

"We didn't talk about a salary."

Amos named an hourly rate that she suspected was too high for a secretary with no experience. Still, she wasn't in a position to turn it down, so she said, *"Danki."*

"Like Lucas, you can eat in the canteen for free—all our employees do. I've already given Isaac's name to our *youngies* who work with the children. They'll pick him up when school is out and bring him here where he can do homework or play in our park until you're done for the day."

"That is all very generous." Hope almost didn't push the point, but she knew that it would rankle her like a small rock in a shoe if she didn't ask. "How do you pay a good wage, offer free food and childcare, and still run a profitable business?"

Instead of brushing off her question, Amos took his time considering it. "Our business model is dependent on earning a profit. As you can see, we have the modern conveniences usually associated with *Englischers*—phones, electricity, et cetera. We haven't upgraded to computers yet, and I'm in no hurry to do so."

He gaze moved to the door, then the window.

What was he seeing?

What was he thinking?

"I suppose that will be Gideon's decision."

"It's a difficult thing, I would imagine."

"What is?"

"To hand over your life's legacy."

Amos fidgeted with his glasses, picked up the pen, then set it parallel to the pad of paper.

"The truth is that this market has been more successful than I could ever have imagined. I try to put that success, that profit, where it belongs. I try to give it back to the employees in ways that are helpful. A higher salary is one way to do that, but things like childcare and food are important perks as well. Those same benefits help to lower everyone's stress, which in turn makes them better employees."

"Okay. That makes sense."

He hesitated, and then the grin she was becoming accustomed to was back.

"So, you want the job?"

"I do."

And she did. This was a kind of business that she'd never worked in before. She'd cleaned houses, ran a register in a bakery, even been a waitress when she was younger. This would be—a challenge. Her mind thought of the towering stacks of paper. She'd never been a secretary before, but she knew her alphabet well enough. She suspected there was more to it than that, but she'd figure it out.

The doubting voice that sometimes pushed its way into her thoughts spoke up. *What if you can't do it? What if you mess it up?*

And then she thought of John heading off to work early.

And Isaac hoping to bring home the class rabbit.

And Lucas so unsure about the hows and whys of life.

She thought of the bills that would need to be paid, and the clothes that would need to be bought. Winter was always hardest, but they had a good long time before then. If they all worked hard, they would make it. If this town would give them a chance, maybe they could stay and put down roots.

"It's certainly a lot of work, but I'm happy to give it my best." Which was true. What Hope didn't voice was her growing conviction that perhaps working at the market was just the thing that she needed to get her mind off her own troubles.

She couldn't follow John around. She couldn't solve Lucas's problems. Isaac was the only one she had much influence over. She would find a way to do this job well. She'd learn from Amos and squirrel away as much money as she could. She'd send part of it—certainly not all of it, but part of it—back to Lancaster.

She'd be grateful for the chance to work.

Even if it only lasted until July 1.

Chapter Three

On Wednesday morning, Amos's eyes popped open thirty minutes before his alarm was due to ring. He thumbed off the alarm, made sure the clock was wound and replaced it on the nightstand beside his bed.

By the time he was dressed for work and sitting at the kitchen table, the sky was lightening. This house was too big. Too quiet. He couldn't fathom being in it all day long. One of his girls should move into it, but no one had jumped at the idea when he'd suggested it two weeks earlier.

Becca and Gideon had been the first to marry. The main house had been full back then, and Gideon had just begun getting on his feet financially. They'd built a home across the front lawn, one close enough that they could smell what the other was cooking for dinner. Many nights they did, in fact, eat together.

Eunice and Zeb had settled into Zeb's old family house. That made sense because there was plenty of work for Zeb to do on the family farm. He'd married, moved to Lancaster, had a son, and then his wife had died from cancer. He'd moved back to Shipshewana a bit lost and unsure of his future. Then he'd fallen in love with Eunice—both Zeb and Josh had. It hadn't made sense for their small family to move when they'd had a perfectly good place to live.

Amos's two youngest girls, Ada and Bethany, had married brothers—Ethan and Aaron. Ada and Ethan had one boy, Peter, who would turn a year old soon. Bethany and Aaron had a daughter who was nearly four and a son who had recently turned six months. Both families lived on the old King farm, and they had expanded the buildings on the property to accommodate everyone. They'd built another house that was connected to the original by a breezeway. The homes on Huckleberry Lane always made Amos smile. His girls belonged there.

Which only left Sarah. His oldest *doschder* had married Noah Beiler. Noah had spent some time away from Shipshewana when he'd been incarcerated in Illinois. His parents were overjoyed and filled with relief and gratitude when he was allowed to return home. Now, Sarah, Noah and their new baby girl, Grace, lived on the family farmstead. The older Beilers had spent many years missing their son, praying he'd return home, believing that *Gotte* still had something *gut* in the future. Sarah had taken care of the family home for years. Asking Sarah and her family to move back home might make sense, but it would certainly cause heartache for Noah's parents.

Amos was, for all practical purposes, stuck with it.

So, what was he to do in the big old house that was stuffed to the rafter with memories? Over the years, the bitter memories had receded. Did he still miss his wife? Of course he did. But she had died more than twenty years ago. He'd built a life here. Raised his girls. And now it was time for him to step aside, to hand over the reins of the business and the farm and the home.

But no one needed the home.

Except the Lambrights. Amos could imagine Isaac running through the fields, a dog at his heels. He could even see

John working in the fields. Lucas he wasn't so sure about. Would the boy be happier in a larger home, or would he feel just as lost? And then there was Hope. She struck him as the kind of woman who knew how to turn a house—any house—into a home.

Perhaps he should rent it out as an Amish B&B. The thought brought a smile to his face and helped to banish the gloomy despair that so often tried to sneak up on him.

He rinsed his cup, washed and rinsed the dishes from his breakfast of oatmeal and fruit, and walked to the barn. Even stepping outside caused him a bit of sadness. How many years had their old mutt, Gizmo, met him with a wagging tail and a mischievous glint in his eyes. Gizmo had passed quietly, lying by the heater in the kitchen on a bed lined with blankets that had been given to him over the years.

He missed the company of a dog, but again…did it really make sense to get one now? He tossed that question back and forth as he walked across the yard and into the barn.

"You're up early today, Amos." Gideon was already tending to the horses.

"Oh, *ya*. I suppose I am."

Gideon paused midway to the feed bucket. "Are you sleeping okay?"

"I'm fine, just had enough rest I suppose. Thought I'd head in early."

"I didn't get to talk to you last night. How did things go with Hope?"

"Very well. I think she'll do a *gut* job. It'll probably take her a month just to clear off the desk."

"How did we let things slip so far?"

"Kicked the can down the road, I suppose."

Gideon nodded, satisfied with Amos's answer. Then he

snapped his fingers and asked, "Did you assure her that we'd find a permanent place for her, one way or the other?"

"I didn't."

"Because—"

Amos had trouble articulating why he hadn't done that. The truth was, when he was around Hope, his thoughts often flew out the window. He settled for saying, "I had the sneaking suspicion that it would turn on the waterworks."

Gideon tilted his head and waited.

"Plenty of folks have begun donating things. It can be overwhelming, I think, to be in the position of receiving help—even when you need it. I thought I'd let her get acclimated before we talk about what may happen in the fall."

"Okay. That makes sense."

Amos harnessed Peanut to his buggy. He was about to climb up into it when he asked about Lucas.

Gideon didn't answer immediately. He scratched under his chin and stared up at the barn loft. Finally, he admitted, "The boy seems determined to be unhappy."

"Ya?"

"Offered him his choice of spots to work. He shrugged at me, then Aaron walked in saying he could use some help in the Backyard Barnyard…" Gideon spread his hands out in front of him, as if to say he'd done his best.

"So he's shoveling poop."

"Cleaning out stalls too. Grooming the animals. It's not all bad." Gideon grinned. "Maybe he'll find he likes it."

"But you don't think so."

"At this point in his life, I don't think Lucas Lambright is going to like anything."

"He'll outgrow it." Amos tried to sound more confident than he felt. Something about Hope's middle child suggested the boy was struggling. He had no idea why or what to do about it, so he reiterated, "Nearly all *youngies* find their way over or around that particular speed bump of discontent."

"Hopefully."

He drove to work wondering what he could do for the boy, but he came up with no ideas. He'd ask Ezekiel when they met for breakfast on Saturday. Then he remembered. Saturday was the workday. He wouldn't have much opportunity to have a private word with Ezekiel. Perhaps he should make time to visit his friend before then.

Having arrived early, he made himself a cup of coffee and sat behind his desk with the accounting books. He spent the next hour going over the numbers. Gradually, he became aware of the hustle and bustle of people arriving, and then he looked up to see Hope standing in his doorway.

She wore the same dress she'd had on the first time he'd met her, but she looked different. It seemed that some of the worry was gone from her expression. He'd actually thought she might turn down the job the day before, but now she was smiling, calling out, *"Gudemariye,"* and asking if there was anything he needed.

"Nein. I'm *gut.* But *danki* for asking."

"Isn't that what a secretary is supposed to do?"

"Perhaps a secretary who can actually find her desk. In your case, I won't expect you to bring me coffee."

Her smile brightened. "Guess I'll get to it then."

She was certainly a hardworking woman. Amos knew a thing or two about that. His own mother had raised a family back in the days when being Plain meant having an outhouse and a wringer washing machine. His wife, Lydia, had single-handedly taken care of their home and four children while Amos had worked extra hours at the market. It had only been when their fifth child, Ada, was born that Lydia had slowed down, and they'd soon learned it was because of cancer. His five *doschdern* were also quite industrious—though that meant different things to every one of them. Eunice loved working on small machinery. Ada was a dreamer, but one who was constantly busy. The other three girls landed somewhere in the middle.

Still, watching Hope Lambright work was a whole other schooling in the power of one motivated person. She arrived at the market as early as was humanly possible considering she first had to walk her youngest son to school. By Friday, he became convinced that she was only taking a fifteen-minute lunch, when he'd twice reminded her that she had a half hour—technically longer since she didn't take a morning or afternoon break.

Amos waited until she'd left to grab a sandwich, then he walked around her office to try to figure out exactly what she was doing. There were stacks of paper and boxes along the perimeter of the room, with yellow sticky notes adhered to the wall above them. He couldn't quite figure out what they meant. He stepped closer to peer at one when Hope walked back into the room and stopped short.

"Thought you'd gone to lunch," Amos said, though he knew that didn't answer the question she was no doubt sorely tempted to ask.

Being polite, she smiled and held up a to-go bag from the canteen. "Decided to eat at my desk." She set the bag of takeout on her desk and walked over to where he was standing. "I guess you're wondering what all these stacks are."

"You're working quite hard, that's for certain. What does H1 mean?"

"Housekeeping, priority."

"Ah. And HL?"

"Housekeeping, but Later—as in not a priority."

"B would be for Barnyard, A for Auction…"

"Right. I looked at the departmental listing of personnel and came up with my main categories."

"Priority means they need it right away."

"As soon as everything is sorted, I'll start on those stacks first."

"The rest can be done later."

"Exactly." She grinned as if he'd offered her a gold star.

Amos leaned closer and lowered his voice. "Didn't find any past-due invoices in there, did you?"

"I didn't. Someone did a *gut* job of pulling out what needed to be addressed in a timely manner."

And now Amos had the oddest sensation that he'd been given that gold star. They stood there, grinning at one another for a moment, and then Hope nodded at her desk. "Sure you don't want half of my sandwich?"

"*Nein*. You eat that. In fact, I should go get something myself."

But he wasn't very hungry, so instead he walked through the vendor booths that were being cleaned and repaired where needed. The market would open in ten days. Usually he was excited about that, but this year he could only think that it might be the last time he would oversee an opening day. Oh, sure, he could stop by after he retired. It wouldn't be the same though.

It seemed that nothing in his life was the same. Everything was changing. More precisely, everything was moving on without him. And he didn't know what—if anything—he could do about that.

The rain started at twenty minutes after four in the afternoon. Hope's gaze kept darting toward the windows, as if she could wish the storm to move on. She'd lived in farming communities all her life. She understood the importance of rain. She could remember the old folks saying, *If it's raining, we ain't complaining.* That was usually the sentiment anyway. Floods were a different matter.

But flooding and farming weren't her problem today.

Walking home in this downpour was. Fortunately, she'd sent Isaac ahead with Lucas when he'd gotten off work at three thirty.

She'd made good progress on the stacks of mail, deliveries and miscellaneous envelopes. Who knew that a business could produce so many sheets of paper? She'd even figured out Miranda King's filing system. The woman had been organized. That organization had stopped more than two months ago. What Hope was looking at—what she was dealing with—was two months of neglect. She sort of relished the challenge.

She did not relish walking home in the rain.

She tapped her fingers against her desk—her clean, well-ordered, dust-free desk. It almost made her laugh to think of how it had looked only four days earlier. She was doing that, basically congratulating herself, and at the same time wishing away the rain, when Amos walked out of his office. She nearly jumped out of her *kapp.*

"Didn't mean to startle you," he said.

"I may have forgotten you were still in there."

"I suppose I was waiting for the rain to let up, not that it will bother my mare, Peanut. She enjoys a good canter in the rain."

Instead of answering, Hope nodded as if she understood and glanced again at the windows.

"I'll walk you out," Amos said. "If you're going…"

What he left unsaid, what was obvious, was that it was time for the office to close. Past time, according to the clock on the wall. Hope gave up on staring at the rain, reached into the bottom desk drawer for her purse and forced a smile. "Indeed it is."

When they reached the front door, she stepped outside with him, and then she stood there as he locked up the building. She wondered if Amos was going to make her explain it to him. He looked at her quizzically, angling his head to the side, then looked out at the rain, then at the ground. When he met her gaze again, there was more than sympathy there— there was a bit of laughter.

That helped her to breathe in and out.

"Not relishing a walk in the rain?"

"Perhaps a light rain, but not—" She inclined her head toward the downpour.

"Stay here. I'll fetch my buggy."

Before she could argue, he was moving off quickly in the direction of the parking area. He didn't bother with an umbrella. Men rarely did, in her experience. At least he was wearing his straw hat. It would dry easily and might even protect him a bit. Fifteen minutes later, he was back, driving the same buggy with the same pretty mare pulling it that Hope had noticed when he'd visited her at the little house on Willow Lane.

She started to dart toward him, but he was out of the buggy, motioning for her to stay where she was. As he walked around the buggy, he popped open a large black umbrella. It wasn't doing Amos much good, as he was plainly soaked, so why was he grinning?

When he reached her side, he extended the umbrella over her. "Shall we?"

"Someone's mother raised them right." She tried to say it lightly. So many days Hope thought she was over the embarrassment of being poor. Then something like this happened and she was right back where she'd started—a middle-aged woman and mother of three who didn't even possess a horse and buggy with which to transport her children. She didn't have a way to stay out of the rain.

"Indeed. Mamm always insisted I keep an umbrella in the buggy for just such an occasion." He held the umbrella over her head as she climbed into the buggy.

She'd thought the short ride home might be awkward. After all, Amos was her boss. But it wasn't uncomfortable at all, maybe because they worked together every day and were becoming used to each other's company. She was looking forward to meeting his wife and his *doschdern*.

"Will you be at the workday tomorrow?" She kept her gaze pinned on the road, hoping her question would sound casual and breezy.

"*Ya*. Wouldn't miss it."

"It's kind of the people from our church, which I haven't even attended yet."

They'd reached her home, and Amos called a gentle "whoa" to the mare. He reached for the umbrella but didn't get out. "I know what you mean. And indeed the community here is kind, but it's more than that, Hope."

She cocked her head, cornered herself against the door of the buggy and waited for him to go on.

"It's what we're commanded to do—be the hands and feet of Christ, *ya*?"

"It is." Her words were soft, even to her own ears.

"Sometimes we do that for those outside our church. My *doschder*, Becca, was involved with MDS mission trips. Are you familiar with them?"

"I am." And now she was answering all of his questions with two-word replies. She resisted the urge to tap her forehead. Maybe she could shake something loose in there. "I haven't had the opportunity to work on a mission trip myself, but many in our Lancaster church went."

"Those trips changed Becca. She returned home, and she shared with us stories of the people she'd met. When she did that, I suppose it changed us all." He smiled but in a sad way. "Maybe I should look into joining an MDS crew once I retire."

"Would you really do that?" Hope wondered if his wife would go with him. He didn't talk about her much, or maybe not at all, but then for many people marriage was private.

"I may. But that's beside my point. On a mission trip, both parties are changed by the grace and love of God—the person receiving and the person giving."

She nodded, understanding that he wasn't merely talking about MDS mission trips. He was talking about the workday that would take place at her home the next morning. Hope found herself blinking back tears. Why was it that when someone was overtly kind to her she felt so emotional?

"Thank you for your hard work this week."

"Amos, you're paying me."

"Yet not every employee is as dedicated as you."

A slow blush started up her cheeks. There was no use trying to stop it. She'd always been a blusher. Just another embarrassment to endure, though her sons loved to tease her about it. Her parents had too. She missed them—missed her *mamm* and *dat*. If they hadn't died, she'd probably still be in Lancaster.

Every night this week she'd woken between 3:00 and 4:00 a.m., wondering if she'd done the right thing. She'd tossed and turned as if moving to Shipshewana were something she could undo, as if she'd even want to. She was tired, and she was overly emotional. The rain continued to fall, a kind man had driven her home, and she had to go into it with three growing boys and only a little bit of food.

She needed a good night's rest.

She needed to be past this beginning part of starting over.

"Thank you, Amos." She opened the door, hopped out and dashed up the walk before he could offer his assistance. She paused to wave before going into the house, raised a hand and was surprised to see he was still waiting there. Making sure she got in safely? She was a grown woman, and Shipshewana was a small, close-knit community. She didn't think anyone would be popping out of the overgrown bushes attempting to snatch her purse.

Still, it was kind of him.

The first thing she saw on walking into the kitchen was the small stack of mail. Her heart nearly stopped when she eyed the Lancaster postmark. Instead of opening it, she stuffed the letter into her apron pocket. The rest of the mail was junk that she tossed into the trash.

She made a dinner out of canned tuna and macaroni and cheese. Someone had dropped off a platter of oatmeal cookies, and all three of her boys were happy to lay waste to them with what was left of the milk. They spent the evening in the living room that held no furniture, sitting on the floor and playing a game of Skip-Bo, something John had thought to pack in his bag.

Long after the boys had fallen asleep, she lay on her sleeping bag, staring up at the ceiling. She tried tossing, which wasn't easy to do. Finally, throwing back the sleeping bag, she stood, retrieved the letter from her apron pocket and the small flashlight from her suitcase. She took both into the bathroom, quietly shutting the door behind her. With trembling hands, she opened the envelope and pulled out the single sheet of paper.

Moving doesn't change what you owe me, what your
husband took from me. Guess you thought I wouldn't
find you. I did, and I will still contact the law if you
don't begin to repay the three thousand dollars that
Daniel swindled out of me. You have thirty days to
make your first payment. Send three hundred dollars,
or I will give your name and address to an attorney.
Edwin Bing

She slipped the sheet back into the envelope, returned to
her room and put the letter in her suitcase with the others.
Edwin Bing wasn't the boogeyman. He was a person struggling the same as she was. *Englisch*, not Amish. Younger
than her by a good fifteen years. She'd only met him once.
It had been enough. He was foolish and arrogant, and he'd
willingly gone along with Daniel's latest scheme to get rich.
That had been the month before Daniel had died. The letters
had begun arriving three months ago. Demanding restitution. Threatening a lawsuit. She still didn't understand why
he was sending them. Why now? Why a full twenty-one
months after her husband had passed?

She couldn't focus on that right now.

She couldn't allow Daniel's mistakes to follow her here.

Hope took in three deep breaths, snuggled into her sleeping bag and tried to focus on the positive. She had so much
to be grateful for—the small house they'd purchased, the
kindness of their neighbors, the jobs they'd been able to
find, Amos.

He was a *gut* man. Her heart wanted to cry out to *Gotte*
and ask why some men were good providers and others struggled. Why some spouses were dependable and others were
not. So many questions, and did the answers really matter?
Life was better accepted as it was than struggled against.

Hope for the best, prepare for the worst, and take what comes with a smile. That had been one of her *dat*'s favorite sayings.

She truly was hoping for the best here in her new home.

She liked to think they'd prepared for the worst, or rather that they were preparing for it.

If they could save enough money for winter…

If they could truly become a part of this community…

If Lucas could mature enough to stay out of trouble…

As for *taking what comes with a smile*, what other choice was there? She wiped away the tears that fell faster than the rain had that afternoon. Her well of worry and sadness was bottomless. But she wasn't a child. She was a mother and a provider and a secretary. The last made her smile, even as she rolled onto her side and tried to ignore the pain in her hip. She was rather old to be sleeping on the floor.

Six months.

If things would go well for six months…

She fell asleep envisioning a house filled with furniture. Cupboards brimming with food. Her boys—happy, fulfilled, safe. And maybe, if things went better than she had any right to hope for, she would even have a friend. She realized with a sudden start that she missed that—the solidness of friendship—more than anything else. She didn't think she would ever marry again. Couldn't imagine anyone wanting to tackle her and her problems. But a true friend, now that would be a blessing indeed.

Chapter Four

Hope thought she had a good idea of what the workday would entail.

Someone would come by the house and evaluate what needed to be done. Check. Ezekiel had stopped by with Saul Gold on Wednesday morning. Saul was the deacon in charge of the benevolence fund. They spent an hour going through the house, up into the attic, walking the small yard and peering into the shed at the back of the property.

Supplies would be ordered and delivered. Check. A delivery truck had pulled up Thursday morning and unloaded enough lumber and paint for several houses.

One of the women would stop by to inquire as to what size clothing her boys wore. Check. Martha Lapp visited with her Friday morning at the market. She had written down shoe and clothing sizes—for the boys and for Hope.

Everyone was kind.

No one acted the least bit surprised at her family's situation.

However, Hope understood their situation was not normal. Few people moved into a home with nothing but two sets of clothing in their battered suitcases. Amish came from large families, and families helped one another out of tight spots. Hope's situation was different in every respect, and she didn't have the inclination or the energy to explain that to everyone. To anyone. Fortunately, no one asked.

She understood what the work day would be like and what conflicting emotions it might bring for her sons. She sat her boys down the evening before—a euphemism if there ever was one since they had no chairs. The three boys sat on one of the mattress-less beds in their room. Hope had been able to completely cover the box springs with old blankets that Ezekiel had brought. She sat on the other box springs and tried to prepare her sons for what was about to happen. She explained that the day would start before dawn, that they would be expected to help, that they should be grateful but not embarrassed.

"It is embarrassing though." Lucas crossed his arms and frowned. "We're the poorest family in town, and everyone knows it."

Poverty and health are better than sickness and wealth.

The words were on the tip of her tongue, but she didn't say them aloud. She knew from experience that her middle son could not be reasoned out of a bad attitude with an Amish proverb.

"We've received help before," John said. "But nothing like this. What gives?"

"There are two main differences between our life in Lancaster and the one we're trying to begin here. The first is that Lancaster is one of the largest Amish communities. Shipshewana, by contrast, is quite small."

"And?"

"And when you're in a small community, people notice needs. Ezekiel was here the morning after we moved in. Stephen Miller offered you a job that afternoon. Amos Yoder came by the next day to offer Lucas a job."

"Shoveling horse poop. Some job." Lucas picked at his

fingernails. "It's not like I want to do that the rest of my life, or even the rest of the summer."

"It pays well, bro." John nudged his brother's shoulder.

Hope added, "Amos will move you to something with more responsibility when you've proven yourself."

"What's the second reason, Mamm?" John looked puzzled. Her oldest was adjusting to the move well. He seemed to enjoy his job, came home every day whistling, put all of his tips in the family's money jar and did so without complaint. "I still don't get it."

"Me neither. Why are they giving us stuff?" Isaac tugged on his right earlobe and looked at Hope with such genuine puzzlement that it caused her heart to ache. She needed to be the one to tell him though. Word traveled, even in small northern Indiana communities. Soon enough, everyone in town would know about Daniel.

"The second reason is that our community in Lancaster had helped us many times. Some of those times John will remember, maybe Lucas, but you were too small, Isaac. Your *dat*, well, he loved you all very much—"

"Had a funny way of showing it," Lucas murmured. "He's the one who left us in this situation."

"Your *dat* didn't choose to die, Lucas. He was young to have suffered from an aneurysm, only fifty-one. But you are correct that he wasn't wise with money. My point is that our old community helped us many times, and after a while I think people lost their enthusiasm for doing good."

That sat between them awhile until Isaac asked, "Will that happen here? Will people get tired of helping us?"

"It won't," Hope answered with as much certainty as she could muster. "The reason it won't happen here is because here, we're going to help ourselves. All that happens tomorrow will be a blessing. It will help us find our footing. But making a life in this community is up to us. We will each do our part, and then we won't need assistance anymore. Hopefully, one day soon, we'll be the ones helping another family."

John nodded in agreement.

Lucas grimaced.

Isaac threw himself into her arms and gave her a nice, tight hug.

Hope thought she was ready for what would occur on Saturday. She thought she understood just how different life in Shipshewana was. She set her little wind-up alarm clock to go off at 4:00 a.m. Hurrying to the kitchen, she realized there was nothing she could do to prepare for the workers. She was nearly out of the coffee someone had given them. She had no ingredients to make baked bread or cookies or muffins. She had nothing to offer these people. She hadn't even received her first paycheck yet.

Instead of dwelling on that sad state of affairs, she walked to the bank of windows that looked out over their backyard. She stood there, waiting on the sunrise, thanking God for her blessings, for her family, for this new start, for people who were willing to help.

She opened her eyes and saw the first rays of morning light spilling across the yard and the trees. She could do this. She could be gracious, accept whatever help was offered, live with the embarrassment. She could do any of those things any number of times if it meant her boys would have a better life.

And then her thoughts were interrupted by the sound of horse hooves, the clatter of buggy wheels, the calls of "*gudemariye*" from one person to another. She expected perhaps half a dozen male workers, maybe even a few women. Nothing could have prepared her for what she saw as she strode to the front of the house and opened the door.

A line of buggies were turning into her front yard as well as the adjacent pasture. She tried to count them, then gave up. Every man and woman nodded or smiled or called out good morning to her as they unloaded their tools, supplies and donations.

John joined her at the door.

"Wow," he said, pulling his suspenders over his shoulders, then turning to grin at her.

By eleven that morning, every room in her house had received a fresh coat of paint. Windows were flung open to usher in fresh air. Screens were removed, cleaned, repaired where necessary and replaced. Rotten boards on the outside of the house had been pulled off and new ones nailed into place. The roof had been patched. Shrubs had been trimmed and the yard had been mowed. The fence around the backyard had been shored up, and a new clothesline had been installed. After lunch, the painting would continue on the outside of the home as furniture was moved into the small rooms.

"It'll hold through the winter," Saul Gold assured her of the patched roof. "Next year we'll look at replacing it, if need be."

She'd been holding back tears all morning, but a few slipped down her cheeks. "*Danki*. You can't imagine what a relief—"

And then she stopped.

Because the list he couldn't imagine was too long.

Hope considered herself an optimistic person, but she had her fears. Her worries of all that might go wrong the next day. Late at night, her mind imagined the worst scenarios—taunting her for what she wasn't able to provide her sons. She didn't share any of those things with Saul. She swiped at her tears and tried to find her voice.

Saul had patted her clumsily on the shoulder and murmured, "We'll talk about what financial help you may need next week. Until then, folks donated a little to help you get started." He set the envelope on the kitchen counter, then beat a hasty retreat.

Hope placed a trembling hand on top of the envelope, closed her eyes and offered up a prayer of gratitude. Why was this so hard? She'd never considered herself a prideful person, but she supposed that could be part of the problem she was struggling with. How did a person humbly accept such a tremendous amount of help?

Hearing footsteps, she attempted to pull herself together when a tall, thin woman joined her at the counter.

The woman held her infant *doschder* in one arm and brandished a cloth diaper with the other. "Use this. It's reasonably clean."

Hope had to laugh at that.

She remembered the days when she'd used a cloth diaper for everything from mopping up spills to wiping tears.

"This is all a lot to take in," she murmured, swiping at her cheeks and moving to the bank of windows that overlooked the backyard—the backyard that was filled with friends she hadn't yet met.

"*Ya.* I imagine it is."

Dishes. Food. Furniture. Mattresses. Clothing. Bedding. Money.

"I used our last dollar to buy this place. Hoped that a new start in a new place could fix what ailed us. I never imagined…"

She stopped because if she didn't, the waterworks would begin in earnest. Instead, she smiled tightly and turned to the woman standing beside her. "I'm being rude. I don't even know your name, and I'm crying on your shoulder already."

"Tears are the heart's way of expressing what we feel when we can't find the words. And I'm Amos's oldest *doschder*, Sarah."

"Oh. Amos has been a real godsend. Do you all have a big family?"

"Bigger every day." Sarah proceeded to point out her four *schweschdern*, their husbands and the children. They were all gathered in Hope's backyard. The women were placing platters of sandwich fixings on tables that had mysteriously appeared. "We gave my *dat* quite the number of sleepless nights."

"I doubt that."

"Oh, we were well behaved…unless you count Eunice's work on people's roofs. She loves to tinker with anything mechanical, regardless how much heartburn it gives the rest of us. Then there's Ada's menagerie of animals, Becca's mission trips and Bethany's quietness, which was a whole different kind of worry." She smiled broadly, kissing the infant on top of her head and switching her to her other shoulder.

"Your *mamm* must be a patient woman. I don't think I've met her yet."

Sarah cocked her head, waited a beat, then said, "My *mamm* died when I was eleven."

Hope's mind blanked for a moment. Amos was a widower? He'd raised his girls on his own? He'd endured the same situation Hope was struggling with? She shook her head, trying to bring her thoughts back to the present. "Sarah, I'm so sorry. I didn't know."

"How would you?" Her smile returned. "For many years I felt like the *mamm* of the family, but now my *schweschdern* have children of their own."

"So you're a *grossmammi*?" Hope teased.

"Definitely not." Sarah again kissed the top of her *boppli*'s head. "Would you mind holding Grace while I…"

She nodded toward the bathroom.

"I'd be happy to." Hope accepted the child into her arms and felt that maternal bliss that she'd known with each of her own boys. Her concerns had been so much simpler then. Keep them dry, fed, safe. When had life become so much more complicated?

Sarah's baby looked up at her with such trusting eyes. Her tiny perfect lips formed an O and one fist waved in the air. Hope thought there was nothing sweeter than a newborn baby. This one smelled like powder and love. Could a baby smell like love? She thought that possibly they could.

When Sarah returned and took baby Grace back into her arms, Hope felt momentarily adrift. She hadn't realized how much she'd missed the comfort that came from snuggling a little one.

"My husband is Gideon," Sarah said. "He's the general manager at the market."

"Oh. I met him—my first day on the job. He's kind and efficient. Amos puts a lot of trust in him."

Sarah laughed again. "It's a bit of a family business. All of us girls worked there at one time or another, and most of my *bruders*-in-law do as well. I hear you're working in the office."

"I am."

"And your middle son, Lucas, also started working there this week."

Hope's shoulders tensed. For many years, when anyone brought up Lucas it was usually with a word of caution or admonition, which might explain why the words Sarah said next put her instantly on the defensive.

"Dat watches new employees pretty closely. Tries to help them settle in. He can seem a bit strict, but he's also fair."

"Okay."

"I don't mean that he's unkind, only that he has high standards for himself and everyone who works with him. He's mentioned how pleased he is with what you've been able to do in the office."

"He has?"

"Yup. I should go and help set out the luncheon." Sarah squeezed Hope's hand, then turned and pushed out the back door, going toward the tables laden with food.

Strict but fair?

High standards?

What did those things mean?

Hope didn't like the sound of it. She knew her son, and she understood that he had an attitude that needed correcting. Handling him was like walking a circus high wire.

Strict but fair.

That sounded like an approaching disaster.

She could talk to Amos, but what would she say? *Go easy on him? His father died only two years ago? He's trying to find his place in this world? Please be kind?*

She wouldn't say any of those things. She was aware that even among the Amish, people had different ways of parenting. Being strict but fair might have worked with five young girls. With Lucas, it was bound to result in fireworks and trouble.

Amos waited until tools were packed up, supplies were stored, and buggies were for the most part headed away from Hope's place. When the only two people who remained were he and Ezekiel, he looked over to his friend, who nodded once. Together, they sought out Hope. She was on the front porch, sweeping off imaginary dirt.

Hope looked exhausted. Amos hadn't seen her sit for more than ten minutes, and that had been at lunch as she'd gulped a glass of water and eaten half a sandwich. Then she'd hopped up and hurried off to help clean paintbrushes. He wondered at the fact she was still standing, let alone sweeping a porch.

She looked up in surprise as they approached, then swiped at hair that was curlier than Amos had imagined, tucking it back into her *kapp* and offering a weary smile.

"Amos and I would like to speak with you and the boys."

"Oh." Her eyes widened, her face paled and her gaze darted left, then right.

What had this woman been through in Pennsylvania that she was as skittish as a newborn colt?

"It's a *gut* thing, Hope." Ezekiel's voice was kind, quiet, low.

"Right. Okay. Let me just…" She set the broom against the wall, then hurried inside, returning with all three boys in tow. As usual, John looked curious, Lucas seemed put out and Isaac hopped from foot to foot.

The sun was near the horizon, and a golden glow bathed the entire family in light as they stepped out onto the porch. Amos saw something then that poked at his heart. He saw himself walking outside one evening not so long after Lydia had passed. Maybe a few months. Possibly more. But he remembered stepping out into a cool evening with Sarah, Becca, Bethany, Eunice and Ada and thinking that this was their life now. That they had each other and would need to find a way forward.

He prayed Hope would find a way forward as well.

"We'll need to walk…" Amos gestured to the adjacent barn and pasture.

Hope met his gaze then. She looked so vulnerable. Amos smiled to assure her that all was fine, and she accepted that reassurance. She nodded once, straightened her posture and turned to her boys. "Let's take a walk."

They spoke of the weather and upcoming summer events. John told a funny story about a Texas tourist who had seemed interested in moving to Indiana, maybe even becoming Amish, until John had reminded him that they had no central heat in the winter.

Hope was the first to notice that there were three buggies parked near the barn and three horses in the pasture. Her mouth opened slightly, and then she pressed her fingers to her lips. Both Amos and Ezekiel noticed her reaction. Ezekiel apparently decided it was best to do this quickly.

"Amos wants you to have the horse and the buggy."

"Oreo is an older mare," Amos hastily added. "But she still enjoys pulling a buggy. She doesn't spook easily on the road, and I think you'll find her to have a gentle nature. Plus, um…she likes peppermints. My girls spoiled that horse with peppermints."

John recovered first. His eyes wide and a smile spreading across his face, he asked, "You're giving us a horse and buggy?"

"We can't accept this," Hope said softly.

But all three boys were already at the fence, studying the mare and high-fiving one another. For once, even Lucas looked happy. Was his sour demeanor a result of constant worry or maybe an overabundance of stress? If so, he temporarily let go of those things as they called out to the mare.

"This is too much," Hope said. Squaring her shoulders, she turned to face Amos and Ezekiel. "I appreciate your kindness. I honestly do, but we can't accept."

Ezekiel only tilted his head and waited.

"We can't," she repeated, more softly this time.

"The real secret of happiness is not what you give or what you receive, it's what you share." Ezekiel chuckled. "My *dat* liked that one. He was right, and I think it applies here. Today wasn't about what people gave or what you and your family received. Today was about a new beginning, one that we gladly share with you, Hope."

Ezekiel reached out, placed a hand on her head and closed his eyes. "May our *Gotte* bless you, John, Lucas and Isaac, as He has blessed our community with your presence." He smiled broadly, then turned to the boys and asked for help hitching his horse to his buggy, leaving Amos and Hope alone.

Amos searched his pockets, finally finding the clean handkerchief he always carried with him and passing it to Hope.

"I'm not much of a crier. At least I never used to be. I don't know what's wrong with me today."

"Today would have been a lot for anyone. The entire past week has been a lot. You started a new job. I heard that place was a real mess." He smiled and added, "Also, I suspect you were exhausted before you ever stepped off the bus."

"True." She swiped her face, then her nose, held the handkerchief out to him, then shook her head and pulled it back. "I'll wash this first. *Danki*, Amos, but the horse and buggy... it really is too much."

Instead of answering, Amos walked over to the pasture's fence, folded his arms across the top, and drank in the sight of the sun's last rays across the pasture, the horse, the boys and his bishop.

When Hope joined him, he continued watching the scene in front of them, but he spoke to her in a soft, reflective voice. "My family has doubled in size in the last few years. Not so long ago, I worried that none of my girls would marry. Now I have five sons-in-law and seven *grandkinner*. *Gotte* has blessed me more than I could have ever imagined possible."

She didn't respond to that. What could she say? Amos realized even as he counted his blessings how that might sound to Hope. Had *Gotte* not blessed her? Had her life always followed a rugged path? How many more years would she struggle? Why was life sometimes so terribly hard?

Hope didn't ask any of those things.

Amos was already learning that she wasn't one to complain.

"I can't even give Oreo the exercise she needs," he said. "You'll be doing me a favor."

Her laughter was full, rich, genuine. "And the buggy? Were you having trouble exercising your buggy, Mr. Yoder?"

He turned and smiled at her, and realized again what a beautiful woman, what a beautiful person, she was.

"Eh. You may not be so grateful for that buggy come winter. It doesn't even have a heater."

"*Danki*, Amos." Her expression turned serious. "For everything. For giving me a job. For giving Lucas a job. For arranging for the washing machine—yes, I realized it was your doing once I understood that Bethany was your *doschder*."

He started to explain that Bethany and Aaron had recently purchased a newer model, but she stopped him with an uplifted hand.

"I appreciate all of it. The workday, the generous donations, the horse and buggy, my job. And mostly, for hiring Lucas." A worried look flashed over her expression then disappeared. "Thank you for your kindness."

"John will know how to care for the mare."

"Yes."

"Lucas should learn to as well."

"I'll see to it."

"And I imagine Isaac will treat Oreo like a pet."

"No doubt. Tomorrow, I'll speak to the owner of this pasture about renting it."

"Already taken care of and paid up through the end of the year. There's feed in the barn, which we'll keep supplied."

She pulled in her bottom lip, closed her eyes, then plastered on a trembling smile. *"Danki."*

"Gem gschehne."

Those traditional words seemed to cement a bond between them. They were both older. They both understood that life could be a struggle. And yet weren't they all in it together? Amos thought so. He hoped she did, too.

As he drove home a few minutes later, he recognized that his involvement with the Lambright family was probably temporary. A single man closer to Hope's age would show interest. She would remarry. The boys would have a true father figure.

But until that happened, he would do what he could. Not a father figure. But a *grossdaddi*. That was it. He'd stand in as a grandfather to the boys, even to Lucas who was already trying Amos's patience at the market. And when Hope remarried, he'd be happy for her. *Gotte* willing, she had many years ahead of her, and she deserved to spend them with someone she loved. Someone who loved her and appreciated what a remarkable woman she was.

He, on the other hand, had entered the final third of his life. Amos wasn't sure what the future held for him, but he doubted that it was a new *fraa* and an instant family. The thought made him laugh, though uncomfortably. Because a part of his heart would have liked to have entertained that dream, even if just for a moment.

Chapter Five

Hope worried that things might be awkward at the church service the next day. As they made their way across the Beilers' parking area, she reminded her boys to be friendly and polite.

"No need to worry about us, Mamm." John smiled and winked.

Isaac was carrying their platter of cookies she'd made the night before. "I'm always polite."

Lucas rolled his eyes.

She needn't have worried about what kind of reception they would receive. The reality couldn't have been further from her gloomy imaginings. She and her family were welcomed warmly. And she felt more comfortable because she wasn't walking into a congregation knowing no one.

The women who had helped the day before said hello, and a few even offered a hand clasp or hug. The men nodded to her with a smile, spoke to John about his job, asked Lucas how he liked the market and inquired as to what Isaac thought about the one-room schoolhouse.

"It's awesome," her youngest replied. "We have a rabbit named Hoppy."

But it was Amos's family that made her feel the most at home. The Yoder women insisted that she sit in the same row as them, passed babies and toddlers back and forth, and treated her like one of the group. When young Abram reached for her and snuggled onto her lap, Hope forgot all her worries.

The service was two hours long, just like in Lancaster. She wondered how her boys were doing on the men's side of the room.

They were doing fine.

Yes, Lucas wore his perpetual scowl, but at least he was awake and participating. John sang along with gusto—she could pick his voice out anywhere. Isaac sat next to Amos's step-grandson, who had recently turned seven. Though there were three years between their ages, they seemed to be getting along well.

She had a slight moment of panic after the service when she and her boys filled their plates with food and turned to look out at the tables and groups. Where should they sit? Maybe they ought to take the little table off to the side that was empty. Or they could try pushing into a table that was half full and risk someone saying they were saving the seats for family members. Before she could choose, Isaac said, "Ada's waving at us."

So, they sat with the Yoders, who laughingly scooched in to accommodate her family of four.

"Two's to tango, and three may good for a game of Skip-Bo. But a full table is just right." Ada smiled and placed a handful of Cheerios on the plate in front of her son, Peter.

"Ada's famous for her sayings," Gideon explained.

"Her mis-sayings," Eunice corrected.

Ada only smiled, then said, "You all are a real piece of blueberry pie."

"Cake," everyone said in unison.

Hope picked at her food, tried to keep straight the names

of each person around her and hoped that her sons felt more comfortable than she did. Why were first days so hard? Had two of the women working the food tables given her the stink eye? Did she misread looks thrown Lucas's way or had people already heard about his trouble in Lancaster? She was slightly overwhelmed by the sheer number of people and the fact that she barely knew anyone. Compared to this crowd, working in the market office was a piece of…blueberry pie.

Soon the young people stood, stretched and took their little ones on a walk. "Helps with the napping," Becca said with a smile.

Hope remembered.

She remembered everything about having young children. Though she suspected her experience parenting had been a bit different than Amos's. She would often take her boys on long Sunday walks to take their attention away from their abject poverty. She didn't see any poverty like that here, but she suspected it did exist. Didn't every group have their poorer members?

"You must be thinking deep thoughts given the serious expression you're wearing." Amos set a small plate stacked with sweets in front of her. "Noticed you missed the dessert table, so I brought you a variety of things."

"I can't eat all of that."

He shrugged. "Then we'll share."

They split the piece of pie—it really was blueberry—in half, each took a peanut butter cookie and jointly decided to save the brownies for later.

"How is your first Sunday going?"

"It's a lot." She glanced to her left, then right, but she couldn't spy her sons.

"The boys are fine." Amos was facing away from the barn they'd had the service in. "John is joining the baseball game. Isaac looks to be trying to catch a frog with a passel of other *kinner*."

"And Lucas?"

"Two other boys just invited him to play Frisbee."

She understood in that moment that Amos didn't miss much. He understood that she worried more about Lucas than the others. He probably even understood what it was like to have a child that you worried about, though his *doschdern* seemed to be living the ideal Amish life. Still, she knew that things weren't always as they appeared. And Amos had mentioned worrying that some of the girls would never marry.

"You don't have to stay here with me," Hope said. He looked up in surprise, and she added, "I mean, if you want to go and sit with your friends."

His look of surprise turned into a slow smile. "Trying to get rid of me, and after I brought you a plate of desserts."

"Which I shouldn't have eaten. Now I'll be tempted to fall asleep."

"You wouldn't be the first." He stood and gathered their dishes. "I'll go slip these into the wash buckets. Then we can walk around the pond…if you'd like, that is."

"Yes, I would." Hope was finding that Amos was easy to be with. He seemed satisfied whether they talked or remained silent. She could use that kind of companionship.

After he'd dumped their dishes, he came back, motioned toward the pond, and it was then she saw that there was a sort of trail around it. They walked through the May sunshine, and Hope relaxed a little. She longed to enjoy the laughter, the camaraderie, the restfulness of a Sunday afternoon.

There was something about Amos that was different from other men she'd known well—which consisted only of her husband and her father. What was it? Certainly wasn't his age, though he was younger than her father and older than

Daniel. Wasn't his looks—blue shirt, suspenders, beard that had gone a little gray, hair cut in their customary style. He seemed... She snapped her fingers. "You're content."

"Say again?" They were halfway around the pond, and Amos stopped, turned toward her and waited.

"I was trying to figure out what's different about you."

"Different?"

"From most men. Or rather, most people. It's that you're content."

A smile crinkled the skin around his eyes. "I am. A good bit of the time I am." His smile dimmed, and they resumed walking. "That's not completely truthful. Lately I haven't been satisfied with life. I've felt somewhat untethered. But today, you're correct. I do feel content."

"Why is today different?"

There was such a weighty pause that she thought he might not answer. Some people preferred to keep friendships superficial. Had she pushed? Had she been intrusive?

He cleared his throat and spread his hands out to include all that was around them. "Maybe today is different because I'm here with my family. I'm not focused on myself, but rather on the sermon, the singing, the Word."

"I understand." Hope's thoughts flashed back to the letters from Edwin Bing. She didn't want to think about that today, so she turned to Amos and smiled. "When I'm home, my own problems loom over me. After the service, which was lovely by the way, and the meal and this nice stroll, which is helping me to walk off those desserts... Well, now those things I focused on last night have faded into the background."

"Indeed."

Hope didn't want to pry, but it seemed that Amos wanted to unburden himself. He was reaching out, and hadn't she been in that position before? That sympathy or empathy caused her to ask, "Why were you feeling untethered?"

Amos motioned toward a bench that had been placed back underneath the boughs of a large maple tree. When they'd sat, he rubbed at the muscles on his neck, then leaned forward and clasped his hands together. "Several reasons, I think."

"Go on."

"I've never been this old before."

"Ah."

"You say that with the youthful exuberance of someone who has not yet celebrated their sixtieth."

"Or even fiftieth."

"Ouch."

"Ouch?"

"I knew there was an age gap between us, but I didn't realize it was so large."

Hope had never thought of age that way. There were children, *youngies* and adults. Perhaps she sometimes divided those around her into younger adults—those just starting their families—and older adults attempting to meet the challenges of parenting and all that brought with it. Amos was acting as if there were demarcation lines at every decade with large Do Not Cross signs posted at the age change. "I'm forty-six, Amos. Definitely, no spring chicken."

"I remember forty-six." He combed his fingers through his beard and glanced at her mischievously. "It was a *gut* year."

"Uh-huh. I would have guessed you were in your fifties. You must have turned sixty recently."

"I did."

"Which makes you fourteen years older than me."

"A lifetime." His voice had turned serious.

"A fourteen-year-old *youngie* might agree with that statement, but I don't."

"Why is that?"

She stared out at the well-tended farm, and for the first time in many years she didn't feel jealousy so much as a growing kinship. "At our age such differences melt away. What matters more is that we are both caring for our family."

"Mine's married off."

"Do they still ask your advice?"

"Of course."

"Still tell you when they've had a good day or a bad one?"

Though his expression had grown somber, a smile tugged at his mouth. "Sarah admitted that she cried over a bottle of spilled milk, if you can believe that one. And Becca mentioned the flowers blooming at the back of her house."

Hope found herself nodding adamantly. "I don't worry when they talk to me. It's when they grow quiet that I want to rush in and fix whatever is wrong."

"Lucas?"

She laughed, though it sounded forced even to her. "Usually Lucas is the one I worry about. Which of your girls has given you the most sleepless nights?"

"Ada, without a doubt." Amos's laugh was rich. Full. They stood and continued their stroll around the pond, and Amos told her about Ada's many jobs, how he'd feared she'd never grow up, how they'd always treated her as the baby of the group.

"Which she was. Right? She's your youngest?"

"Yes, but we probably overdid it. I think all of us were compensating for the fact that she never knew her mother."

"Sarah told me about your wife. I'm sorry for what you went through."

"It was many years ago."

"Old wounds can still hurt at times."

"Quite true." He stopped at the edge of the pond, picked

up a pebble and skimmed it across the water. "What of your husband? How long has he been gone?"

"Daniel passed almost two years ago." Standing in the May sunshine, the sound of children's laughter around her, it was hard for Hope to fully explain the darkness of those days. Instead, she said, "He had an aneurysm. Lucas found him in the barn."

"A hard thing for a boy to go through."

"He was thirteen at the time and already leaping into his *rumspringa*. His *dat*'s death pushed him even further in that direction."

"Is that why you moved here?"

"It's one of the reasons. We all needed a fresh start. That's what I was looking for when I scoured the *Budget* and found the listing for our little house."

"It took a lot of courage for you to move."

She didn't respond to that because the word that came to her mind was *desperation* not *courage*. Raising three boys, providing what they needed, preparing for emergencies, dealing with issues from Daniel's past. Many days, those things towered over her. Courage? Probably not. She settled for saying, "I think that we can do just about anything if we believe it will benefit our children. The problem is that you can never be sure."

You can never be sure.

There was something about the way that Hope had said those five words that poked at Amos's heart. Her countenance had once again grown somber. The worry lines had reappeared between her eyes. He wanted, more than anything, to wipe that worry away. He wanted to make her smile.

"It must be hard, raising three growing boys on your own. It was hard for me to raise five girls."

"Yes."

"Most folks remarry." He looked up at the sky, out at the field, and finally over at Hope. "If your thoughts run in that direction, I could make a few discreet inquiries."

"Whoa. Whoa. Whoa." Hope stopped, looking at him in alarm. "I am not looking for a man to rescue me, Amos."

"Of course."

"We've been on our own for two years, longer if I am being truthful. We're doing just fine."

"I didn't mean to suggest—"

"Apparently you consider yourself quite the matchmaker."

A blush had crept up her face, reminding Amos of a thermometer that was spiking into the red zone.

He cleared his throat. "For my *doschdern*, yes, but—"

"But I'm not your *doschder*."

They'd somehow made it back around the pond to where they'd started.

"Now, if you'll excuse me, I should go help with the cleanup."

He stood there watching after her, wondering how he'd messed up a perfectly pleasant stroll. Of course, that was when Ezekiel walked up. "Something wrong, Amos?"

Amos took his hat off, slapped it against his pants leg as if that would ward off any trouble, then slipped it back onto his head. "Not sure."

"Sounds as if there's a story there."

"Possibly."

Ezekiel's right eyebrow shot up, and he nodded toward two chairs facing the pond. Once they were seated, Amos didn't know where to begin. What had just happened?

Ezekiel attempted to get the conversation rolling with, "You were walking with Hope."

"I was. I thought we were both enjoying a leisurely stroll,

but the next thing I knew, the winds had changed." He raised his hands then let them drop. "She was...well, she was put out with me."

"Hmmm," Ezekiel said, which with the good bishop was paramount to saying *tell me more*.

"We were talking about the challenges of being a single parent, and I offered to make some discreet inquiries if she were interested in remarrying."

"What did you say exactly?"

"I said that many people remarry. She didn't respond to that, and then I said...well, I suppose I said I could attempt to find a match for her."

"Uh-oh." The good bishop appeared to be fighting a smile.

"She then informed me that she didn't need to be rescued—"

"Hope strikes me as a strong, resilient woman."

"And she went on to say that perhaps I wasn't the matchmaker I fancied myself to be."

Ezekiel sat forward, elbows braced on his knees, hands over his face. His shoulders shook for a moment, and then he sat up straighter, smiled at Amos and motioned for him to go on.

"Nothing else to say, and I wouldn't want to throw you into another laughing spasm."

"Laughter is good for the heart and the soul. I'm sorry if my amusement offended you."

"Eh." Amos couldn't work up enough indignation to label himself offended. This day was beginning to wear him out. He needed to conserve his energy. "I suppose it may seem funny from your perspective."

"What? That you would suggest a bright, nice-looking woman who has been in town for just more than a week may need help attracting a man?"

"I didn't mean it as an insult."

"I'm sure you didn't." Ezekiel studied him a moment, then asked, "Mind if I offer some advice?"

"Would it stop you if I did?"

"It would."

"Then I don't mind."

"Perhaps you fell into the role of matchmaker quite naturally, and you have been successful. Five weddings in less than five years is a *gut* record."

"But—"

"But Hope isn't your *doschder.*"

"Something she was quick to point out." Amos frowned, stared at the pond and then asked, "So, you think I offended her?"

"Perhaps."

"She did point out that she's been on her own for two years and has gotten on just fine."

"Right. She's a—"

"Strong, independent woman," they said in unison.

"I think the point I want to make, which I'm sure you now realize, is that Hope Lambright isn't an abandoned pup. She's a person."

"Of course." Amos sighed deeply. He felt all of his sixty years in that sigh. This sudden realization that he'd been guilty of overstepping a boundary—he'd experienced it before. "Every one of my girls was offended when I meddled, but in the end it all worked out."

Ezekiel nodded in agreement. "But back to my advice… perhaps it's time to focus on your own happiness."

"I don't follow."

"What is your heart telling you?"

"My heart?"

"Are you interested in Hope…personally? Romantically?"

Amos had to force himself to remain in his chair. This conversation had gone from absurd to ridiculous. "I'm fourteen years older."

"My *dat* was fifteen years older than my *mamm*. It's not unusual among older folks. It's definitely not unusual in Plain communities."

There had been a twelve-year difference between his own parents. Amos had forgotten about that. But Ezekiel was misreading this entire situation. "Hope Lambright is most certainly not interested in me."

"How do you know?"

"How do I know?"

"Have you asked her?" Ezekiel waited for an answer. When none came, he added, "Perhaps you hurt her feelings when you offered to find her a match."

"How would that hurt her feelings?"

Ezekiel shook his head as if he were a schoolteacher frustrated by a student. Finally, he waved toward the area where the buggies were parked. "It would be akin to saying, 'That old buggy over there isn't fine enough for me, but perhaps I know a neighbor who would like to have it.'"

"You're comparing Hope to a buggy?"

"I'm making a point—one that I think you understand well."

"I suppose." Amos ran a hand up and down his jawline. "I didn't mean to upset or insult her. Perhaps I should apologize."

Wouldn't you know it, at that moment he looked up to see his former buggy, driven by Hope's oldest son, pull away from the group and down the lane. The Lambright family was headed home. Had she left early because of him?

"Maybe think on it. Pray on it. I'm sure you'll have a chance to apologize at work tomorrow." Ezekiel stood, patted Amos on the shoulder and then walked toward a *youngie* who was calling his name.

And Amos realized his friend was both wrong and right.

He was wrong because Amos wouldn't have an opportunity to apologize the next day. He would be working all day in the vendor stalls, getting things ready to open on Tuesday. Though he supposed if he got up early enough, he could make it to the office before her. Maybe leave a note on her desk? *Nein*. That sounded like something a teenager would do.

Why did he suddenly *feel* like a teenager?

He was excited and worried and a little sick to his stomach.

He stood, searched for his family, told every one of them that it was *wunderbaar* to see them but he thought he'd leave a little early. Maybe catch a nap. Sarah looked at him with concern. Becca kissed him on the cheek. Bethany hugged him, and Ada walked him to his buggy. The *grandkinner* and sons-in-law all waved and called out.

Amos loved spending time with his family, but right now he needed a few hours alone.

He needed to think about what Ezekiel had said. What he had asked.

Was he interested in dating Hope Lambright?

And under that was a question that struck at the center of his heart. He'd loved Lydia with every fiber of his being. They had truly been one. Losing her had been the most difficult moment of his life.

Was that why he had never remarried?

Was he afraid to risk his heart again? And if he was so afraid, then what was he going to do about his feelings for Hope? One thing he knew for certain, as he made his way toward the big empty house he lived in, was that he cared for her.

Or he could.

The question was whether it be worth the risk.

Chapter Six

Hope arrived at work on Monday morning to find a still-warm, freshly baked muffin on her desk. It was in a paper bag stamped *Shawna Rae's Bakery & Café*. When she picked up the bag, because who could resist a warm muffin, she found a note.

I didn't mean to offend.
Glad you are working here.
Amos

Huh. A man who apologized and brought gifts?

That was rare in Hope's experience.

She poured herself a cup of coffee, split the muffin and enjoyed it as she made her day's to-do list. She'd always found a list to be helpful. It kept her focused on what was important and made her feel as if she'd accomplished some things by the end of the day as she crossed off every item. She wasn't above adding something that had already been done so that she could cross it off and feel a bit ahead of her tasks.

She had made good progress the week before.

The most important items had been delivered to the proper department. Now came the harder task of figuring out what needed to be dealt with and what could be trashed. She finished the list, rolled up her sleeves, literally, and set to work.

Four hours later her stomach growled and she realized it was lunchtime. She wondered why Amos hadn't been into the office yet. Then she stepped outside and her mouth gaped open at the sheer volume of activity.

The vendor area was packed with people, carts, and crates of supplies. Music played from someone's radio or cell phone. It was a festive scene, and she couldn't resist walking through the booths rather than picking up lunch. There were twenty-two rows that looked to have twenty, maybe thirty booths each. The merchandise offered for sale included sunglasses, antique toys, clothing, footwear, homemade soaps, outdoor plants, even bird baths.

The vendors appeared to be evenly split between Amish and *Englisch*, young and old, and it seemed that everyone knew each other. As they decorated their booths, she caught snippets of conversation about children, grandchildren, pets, crops and winter vacations. She stopped midway down an aisle lined with booths containing personalized arts and crafts. She closed her eyes and breathed in the smell of fabric and yarn and craft supplies. Did those things have a specific smell? She thought perhaps they did.

She smiled to herself, thinking of how she loved to sew, how using her treadle machine and watching the straight row of stitches had filled her with such satisfaction. There had been a time when she'd thought of opening her own small shop. Then Daniel had lost their savings on a sure thing... what had it been that time? A hand-cranked dog feeder that he was certain would net them a fortune if they could only sell a thousand of them. Daniel had even drawn up plans for national distribution. He'd given their money to the "inventor" with dreams of entering into partnership with the man.

They'd never seen him again and never received the promised boxes of dog feeders.

They'd been so young. So naive.

It was probably at that moment when Hope had accepted that her dream of opening a craft shop would never happen. Then she'd learned she was pregnant with her first child, and she'd felt silly for worrying about such things.

So many years ago.

So many dreams ago.

She was more there than here—more in the past than the present—when she came around a corner of vendor booths and nearly collided with Amos. He was pushing a wheelbarrow that was filled with colorful bags. Each bag was stuffed with pretty paper. Presents?

"Hope." He stopped and swiped at sweat on his forehead. Gesturing toward the line of stalls that stretched before them, he asked, "What do you think of our little market?"

She laughed. "Little?"

"It's grown a bit since I first started here." Cocking his head, he nodded toward the wheelbarrow. "Want to help me pass out welcome bags?"

"I'd love to. Not sure what my boss would think though. I'm supposed to be filing."

His smile grew even more charming. "Much too pretty a day for that. I only have a few dozen left, and we'll end up by the canteen. Have you eaten?"

"Only an apple muffin." She couldn't help laughing. He'd looked so pleased with himself when she'd said *apple muffin*. "The treat and the note were both sweet. *Danki.*"

"Gem gschehne."

They stood there smiling at each other until a small child rounded the corner, ran into Amos, bounced off him, laughed and took off down the aisle. He was followed closely by his mother. "Sorry, Amos. Josiah, come back here right now."

Hope and Amos exchanged a knowing look.

Toddlers could be a handful.

"I'd be happy to help," Hope admitted.

The bags were filled with coupons for free coffee at the canteen, a complimentary pretzel at JoJo's, a welcome-back card that Hope had unearthed the week before, discount coupons for various booths, informational pamphlets, several pieces of candy and a business card with Amos's cell number.

"A cell phone, huh?" Hope wagged the card back and forth. They'd had one bag left over and had taken it with them into the canteen. Now they were sitting in a corner booth, having shared a small pizza. "You Shipshe Amish are quite modern."

Amos nodded in agreement. "But the number rings through to a flip phone...no internet."

"Oh, no problem then." Hope slipped the card back into the pretty bag. "Some folks in Lancaster had phones. Sort of depended on your business and whether the bishop agreed that you needed one."

"Same here. Our *youngies* now...they all think they want one."

"How does Ezekiel deal with that?"

Amos shrugged. "It's their *rumspringa*. Most of our young people have jobs at one of the local businesses. If they want to spend their money on toys, if their parents are okay with it, then he doesn't intercede. More often than not, the cell phones end up being left in a horse stall or a buggy, their charge completely gone and the person who purchased it no longer interested."

"No harm, no foul."

"Pretty much."

"I've never had a phone," Hope confessed. "Of course, I never needed one either."

"I suppose I'll be passing mine on to Gideon, since he'll be the one in charge."

"Yet one more change."

"Exactly." Amos leaned forward. "Someone reminded me yesterday that I'm probably not as old as I occasionally feel."

"Wise person."

"I think so."

There was an awkward pause as Amos grinned at her and Hope looked at him, then away, then back at him again. She wondered what was happening between them. Was something happening?

They stood, bussed their table and stepped back out into the afternoon sunshine. Hope was about to thank him for a nice lunch break and trot back to the office when Amos turned to her.

"I am sorry about yesterday, Hope. I didn't mean to presume or offend, and I understand you don't need my help with your social life." He looked her in the eyes as he apologized. He waited for her response.

She thought that Amos must have been a *gut* husband. "Apology accepted," she said softly.

"Gut." Amos stuck his hands in his pants pockets, glanced left and right, and nodded in the opposite direction from the office. "Gideon probably needs my help somewhere. I guess I'll go find him."

"And I have filing to do."

Both hesitated, as if they didn't want to walk away. Then a teenage boy dashed up, breathless, and said, "We lost one of the donkeys from the Backyard Barnyard. Gideon said you'd know where to find him."

"I just may."

Amos waved goodbye, and Hope turned toward the offices.

Maybe it was the sugar from the muffin or the carbs from the pizza, but Hope was feeling...well, hopeful. She felt an optimism that she hadn't experienced in quite a while. And there was something else. For the first time in a long time, she felt seen.

When you were a young mom, most people saw your children.

When you were a widow, most folks saw your situation.

It had been a long time since anyone had looked at her and seen her—a forty-six-year-old woman who was doing the best she could every single day.

But Amos had seen her.

She wasn't completely sure whether it was wise or not, but she liked the fact that he had. And she couldn't help wondering what might happen next.

On Tuesday, Amos left a canning jar filled with spring flowers on Hope's desk. He'd woken early, as he so often did these days. Instead of brooding over a second cup of coffee, he'd taken a walk through the fields as the sun rose. He breathed in the newness of the day and appreciated the simple beauty of sunrise dawning across the land. He spied the flowers along the fence line and realized that he might have overlooked them just a few days before.

He'd seen them and thought of Hope.

It was opening day at the market, and he barely stepped foot in his office other than dropping off the flowers. The crowds were even better than they had anticipated, and the day progressed smoothly. Amos enjoyed every moment of it, though his mind kept slipping back to the canning jar full of flowers. Would she think him too presumptuous? Would she find it odd that her boss left flowers on her desk? Had he overstepped?

He worked until past closing and only saw her as she was leaving for the day—Isaac walking beside her, explaining whatever he was saying with both hands. No sign of Lucas, but he'd probably walked home earlier. Hope waved to Amos, and later he found a thank you note on his desk.

Wednesday, he again asked her to lunch.

"On the second day of the season? Don't you need to stay here and…oversee things?"

"I'm going to trust that my number two—"

"Soon to be number one—"

"Has things under control."

They both ordered the bottomless salad from the local deli.

Thursday, when the market was quiet and the vendor stalls were closed, he asked her to go with him to visit one of their elderly vendors who wouldn't be returning. "Esmerelda King weaves rugs and such. She's been a vendor at the market for many years. Last fall, she broke her ankle and moved in with her *schweschder* in Middlebury."

"She's still there?"

"*Nein*. She came back at the first of the year and by March she'd made the decision to move permanently. Esmerelda is eighty-three years young. She found she enjoyed the community in Middlebury and liked living with family. She's joined a book club and a walking club."

"Wow."

"I think you'll enjoy meeting her."

When they arrived at Esmerelda's farm, an old-fashioned loom was being loaded into an *Englisch* moving truck. Esmerelda was overseeing the movers, reminding them the loom was "likely older than their *mammi*," and to take special care with it. She greeted Amos warmly, seemed happy to meet Hope and invited them to the porch for a cold drink.

"I only have soda," she admitted, opening a small cooler, and moving around the ice. "Regular, root beer, or orange."

"What a treat," Amos said. "I'll take a root beer."

"Given that smile on your face, I'm guessing it's been a while since you had a sugary beverage. I suspect those girls of yours are watching what you eat and drink."

"They are indeed."

"Amos had a heart scare a few years," Esmerelda said to Hope.

"Minor," he quickly added.

"It was a wake-up call for his *doschdern* though."

"Indeed. There's barely a sweet thing in my house, and I eat more salad than a rabbit."

Hope reached over and patted his hand. "It's because they care, Amos." To Esmerelda, she said, "I'll have an orange drink if you don't want it."

"I have two."

They popped open the cans, sat in the rockers and Esmerelda shared the brief version of her history in Shipshewana. "Born here. Married here. Had my children here. But my *schweschder* married and moved to Middlebury, which seemed far away back in the day."

"Seven miles to the west." Amos nodded as if to testify to the truth of the next town being *far away*. "Funny how things feel closer now, more accessible."

"I've visited throughout the years, more frequently now that we have drivers who will take us there."

"How long have you lived alone here?" Hope asked.

"Too long. I probably stayed too long, but the memories—" Instead of looking melancholy, Esmerelda smiled brightly and waved toward a stand of trees. "My memories are as thick as the leaves on those trees. A place can hold so much of our past, maybe of our heart, that it feels as if we belong to the land and the land belongs to us. In truth, this land belongs to no one."

Esmerelda laughed. "You look surprised. It's true though. I may hold the deed to the land, but no one can really own it. These fields were here before the Potawatomi people arrived, and it will be here long after you and I are gone. We may grow to love a place, but there still can come a day when you know it's time to move on."

"Yes," Hope said. "That's how I felt. When I left Lancaster. It was time."

"And I will pray that your years in Shipshe will be rich with love, friends and memories."

Even to Amos, it felt like a blessing.

Before leaving, they saw a few of the rugs Esmerelda had made that had yet to be packed.

Fingering one of them, Hope asked, "Did you sell the loom?"

"Oh, no. I'm having it moved to my *schweschder*'s place. She has one of those she-sheds out back that will be a perfect place for me to continue my work."

"Your rugs are beautiful."

Amos thought that Hope seemed especially interested in the process as well as the product. When they were in the buggy again and headed back toward the market, he asked her about it.

"Oh, yes. I love everything that has to do with creating something. By that I mean yarn and fabric."

"You're good with both?"

"I suppose I am." She shook her head, but smiled as she did so. "There are blessings to being poor. I learned to buy old sweaters at garage sales and frog them back."

"Frog?"

"It's the sound the yarn makes when you—" She mimed pulling on a string.

"And you make something new from that?"

"Wash it first, let it dry in the sun, then wind it up and create something new. It's the ultimate form of recycling."

He laughed at that. "Sounds like you found a way to make do."

"Yes." She grew pensive for a moment, but then her smile reappeared. "Yes, both myself and my boys have certainly learned how to make do."

The rest of the drive was spent in a companionable silence. Why was he so comfortable with this woman? He hadn't been alone in a buggy with a woman in years, yet he didn't feel at all awkward. In fact, he was a bit disappointed when the market came into view.

On Friday he took her for an afternoon treat.

"Where are we going?"

"It's a surprise."

"You're going to get me in trouble with my boss."

"Doubtful." He felt like a young scholar cutting class as they climbed into his buggy. The day was pleasantly warm, Hope looked charming in a blue dress—he'd noticed that she rotated between a dark gray, dark green and blue. He thought the blue was his favorite because it matched the color of her eyes.

He let the suspense build for a few blocks before he asked, "Do you like ice cream?"

"Yes." She leaned forward, glancing left and right. "Are you taking me to a dairy? Because it doesn't look as if there's an ice cream shop out here."

"Be patient."

"Usually that's not a problem, but—" Hope scrunched

her face, then pointed and laughed when she saw the giant Howie's Ice Cream sign.

He hadn't really looked at it in years. It was very—bright. The letters that spelled "Howie's" were blue against a yellow background. "ICE CREAM" was printed in all caps, magenta colored and quite large. "The sign is mainly for *Englischers*. Amish have been coming here for years."

Both chose a small nonfat yogurt. They took the treats to one of the picnic tables and sat watching families—Amish and *Englisch*—drive in, park, order their treats then settle around picnic tables.

"I'm already learning that Shipshe is a special place." Hope wagged her head left toward the family of three *Englischers*—mom, dad and toddler, then right toward a family of six Amish—*mamm*, *dat* and four children who looked to be between the ages of three and fourteen. "This seems like a *gut* town for families."

"It is."

"And you seem to get along well with your *Englisch* neighbors."

"Indeed." Amos scooped out a spoonful of the raspberry yogurt and savored it. "I think a lot of the credit for that goes to Ezekiel. He's reminded us constantly over the years that we're called to treat others with kindness and love…to treat everyone as we would our brother."

"And yet remain separate?"

"Which is sometimes the difficult part. We don't want to seem proud or as if we are somehow better, holier than others. We're simply following the path that *Gotte* has chosen for us. It doesn't mean that path is for everyone."

"Amos Yoder. You could be a writer. Beautifully said."

He started to say something, stopped himself, then pushed forward. What was he waiting for? He was sixty years old.

He didn't have the luxury of assuming he'd have unlimited chances.

"You're easy to be around, Hope."

"Oh." She looked up in surprise, her little plastic spoon filled with chocolate yogurt nearly to her mouth. Setting it down in the cup, she said, "Thank you. That's a kind thing to say."

"It's an honest thing to say."

She looked a bit flustered, as if she didn't know how to respond to that.

In for a penny, in for a pound. Amos could hear his mother's voice—and it gave him the courage to say the rest of what was on his heart.

"I'll admit I was baffled by your reaction to my suggestion last Sunday—when I offered to make discreet inquiries if you had a mind to date or possibly marry again." When she started to defend herself, he held up a hand. "I'm no longer baffled. Ezekiel set me straight on a few things."

"You spoke to Ezekiel? About us?"

Amos nodded. "He's more than my bishop. He's also my close friend."

"Oh." She set the half-finished cup of yogurt to the side, crossed her arms on the picnic table and waited for him to continue.

"Ezekiel suggested it might be time to focus on my own happiness. That's a thought that hadn't occurred to me. For so many years now, my happiness has been tied up in my *doschdern*. But…they don't need me in that way anymore."

"They do still need you though—in other ways. And they still love you—that's plain to anyone who sees your family together."

"You're right, and I understand that. But I also think that

maybe I was choosing to butt into other people's business rather than deal with my own."

"Wow."

"Yeah. It's been a week of revelations."

"How do you plan on doing that? How does a person even start focusing on their own happiness?"

"By listening to my heart." He pulled in a full deep breath, feeling more vulnerable than he had in a long time. "I know you're new to town. You're just settling in and getting your feet on solid ground. But I'd like to know…that is, if you'd be interested…"

He stopped, nearly laughed because Hope's look of confusion was turning into a slight, gentle, beautiful smile.

"I was wondering if you'd like to go out with me tomorrow."

She didn't even hesitate. "I would love that, Amos."

"Ya?"

Her smile dimmed slightly and her eyes became more serious. There would never be any doubt wondering what Hope Lambright was thinking or feeling—both her thoughts and feelings played across her face like an *Englisch* television show. One only had to pay attention.

"To be clear," she said, "because what's the use of being vague at our age…you're asking me on a date."

"I am."

His heart paused for the millisecond it took Hope to go on, which was impossible. His heart didn't actually skip a beat. He wasn't a *youngie* experiencing love for the first time. But he'd put himself out there, and it was unsettling and exciting at the same time.

"Then I accept."

"Simple as that?"

"Simple as that."

He felt like throwing his hat in the air. Felt like letting out a whoop. Felt, inexplicably, much younger. He fully understood that he was stepping out on a limb here. They both were. They had a *gut* thing going. She was an excellent secretary, and he thought they could be close friends.

But Amos wanted more than friendship.

And he was okay with wanting more.

Maybe he'd been stuck for a very long time, and—without understanding why—he was ready to move forward. He was ready to allow his heart to make decisions.

Chapter Seven

It had been a long time since Hope had been on a date. At the age of twenty-five, she'd been a bit older than most Amish women when they married. Her *dat* had been ill, and she'd been an only child. There'd been no one else to help her *mamm*. So she'd waited. She'd stayed. And then, a year after her father passed, she'd married Daniel.

There had been the occasional casual date when she was nineteen and twenty, but then everyone started pairing up and the dates had become few and far between. She'd missed her chance, or that had been what she'd worried about. Daniel had seemed like a lifeboat in a storm.

Now she was stepping out with Amos, which reminded her of those other dates but at the same time felt different. Hope thought that she and her boys were doing pretty well on their own. She wasn't looking for a lifeboat. She would like a little companionship though—maybe some laughter, a bit of adult conversation, a chance to lay down her responsibilities, even if it was only for one hour.

"Are you sure you don't want me to go with you?" Isaac asked. They'd made Play-Doh at school, and he was mashing his thumb—over and over—into a blue glob of the stuff. "I'd be so quiet you wouldn't even know I was there."

Before she could think of an answer, John piped in. "Can't

leave me here alone, little *bruder*. I need someone to walk to town and eat pizza with me."

"I love pizza!" Squish went the Play-Doh under the palm of his hand. "Can we play Frisbee before we go?"

"Sure can, but I have to warn you—"

"You're a pro. Right." Isaac tidied the Play-Doh into a neat square, hugged Hope, then snatched the Frisbee from the counter. "Sorry, Mamm. Can't go with you."

And he was off, running into the backyard to practice throwing the green disk into the sky—and hopefully not onto the roof.

"Thanks for that," Hope said.

"No problem. I'm glad you're taking a few hours for yourself."

"And you're sure that you didn't have something…social…planned?"

John ran his hand up and around the back of his neck as a smile tugged at the corner of his lips. "There are a few girls that I'm interested in, but I haven't worked up my courage to ask them out yet."

"Seriously?"

"About the interest or the courage?"

"Both."

"Then yes. I'm serious."

Hope had been pawing through her handbag, more for something to do than any other reason. Now she rested her back against the kitchen counter and studied her oldest son. He had turned into a young man when she wasn't paying attention. When had that happened? Last week? Last year?

"It's *wunderbaar* that you've found someone you like, John. And it's commendable that you're taking things slow. Just don't take them too slow."

John's eyebrow arched. "Sounds like there's a story there."

She was facing toward the living room windows and saw Amos pull up in front of the house. "There is. And I'd be happy to share it later. Keep an eye out for Lucas?"

"Of course."

"It's just that I—"

"Worry. I know. But don't—not tonight anyway. Try to have fun." He beamed as if he were the one going out for a carefree evening and walked her to the front door.

"Amos, *gut* evening."

"How are you, John?"

"Well."

"How do you like your job?"

"Actually, I enjoy it more than I thought I would. It's interesting speaking to tourists about our lives and hearing about theirs."

Amos nodded, then smiled at Hope. "Ready?"

"I am." She turned back to John. "When Lucas shows, ask him to stay in."

"Don't worry about anything, *Mamm*."

Which was probably easier said than done, but she was going to try. She and Amos hadn't talked about what they would do on this first date. She'd thought they'd probably go to one of the restaurants in downtown Shipshewana since there was only so far you cared to travel in a horse and buggy. Even for nearby towns, most Amish hired a driver. When Amos drove the buggy through Shipshewana, then turned north, her curiosity piqued.

"Ooh, I haven't been this direction yet."

"I keep forgetting that you're new here."

"Just more than two weeks," she reminded him.

"It's commendable how well you and your boys have fit in, especially in such a short time."

She thought of sharing her worries about Lucas, that he

might have fit in too well, too quickly and with the wrong kids. But this night wasn't about Lucas. It was about her and Amos, and she was determined to enjoy it.

"Don't keep me guessing. Where are we going?"

Amos grinned. "What's the matter, Hope? Don't you like surprises?"

"As a matter of fact, I do."

They spoke of spring, of the crowds they'd had at the market the week before, and of what summer would be like in Shipshewana.

When she caught sight of blue water, she clapped her hands. "I didn't know there was a lake out here."

"Lake Shipshewana. Like the town, the lake is named after a Potawatomi chief. As far as scholars have been able to determine, the Native people were force-marched out of the area in the autumn of 1838."

"I've read a little about those forced marches. They were truly terrible."

"Indeed. Chief Potawatomi made his way back to Shipshewana in 1839 and died in 1841. There's a nice monument on the other side of the lake. It helps us to remember and honor the local Native people as best we can."

Hope supposed history was full of such heartbreaking stories, though it was hard to reconcile with the happy scene in front of her. She could see a few families enjoying picnics, a *dat* fishing with his children, and an *Englisch* family walking two large dogs. Amos directed his pretty mare, Peanut, into a parking area filled equally with cars and buggies.

"This restaurant only opened last fall," he said. "Haven't been here myself so I'm taking a bit of a risk trying out a new place on you. But I have heard the food is delicious."

As they walked toward the picturesque restaurant on the banks of Lake Shipshewana, Hope's nervousness fell away like an old shawl that she didn't need or want anymore. The light breeze lifted her spirits, and the westerly sunshine warmed her soul. A hostess asked if they wanted to sit indoors or out.

"Is outside okay with you?" Hope asked.

"Sounds perfect."

The table they were escorted to had a lovely view of the water. The outdoor seating area was decorated with potted plants and several bubbling fountains. Twinkling lights had been strung haphazardly across the space, giving the area a homey feel. Soft music played over hidden speakers.

"This is *wunderbaar*, Amos. What a treat."

"You deserve a treat, Hope." The waitress brought them water and menus. When she'd left, Amos leaned forward and said. "Not many women—or men for that matter—could move a family, set up a new house, start a new job, and still maintain a cheery disposition every day."

"Don't put me on a pedestal. Just yesterday, I threatened to ground my boys for life if they didn't learn to hang their wet towels on the bathroom towel rack."

"Ah, teens."

"Pretty much sums it up."

Amos ordered grilled fish on a bed of fresh rice with a side of broccoli. Hope opted for the fried fish and French fries. "Yours is healthier," she admitted.

"And yours looks a tiny bit tastier." Amos gave her a look, and Hope started laughing.

"Want to split half and half?"

"Do I ever!"

The evening proceeded like that. She thought she might feel awkward. She thought they might run out of topics to talk about. But neither of those things happened. She didn't know if it was the outdoor location or that they knew each other well from working together, but she felt comfortable with Amos. She felt happy.

"You're smiling again," Amos said as they walked toward the tranquil water.

The sun was setting and reminded Hope of a giant red ball about to bounce against the edge of the Earth. Instead it slipped past the horizon—soundlessly, smoothly, completely.

She turned back toward him. "I'm smiling because I've had a nice evening."

"As have I."

"Thank you, Amos."

"I should be thanking you."

Maybe in a small part of her mind, or her heart, she had wondered if anything would happen this evening to give her goose bumps. She'd felt childish even having that thought. Wasn't it enough that she was with a nice man, a man she liked and respected, and she was enjoying a wonderful evening away from her responsibilities?

As they walked around the lakeshore, they passed into a more secluded spot. Hope turned toward Amos to say something about the bird she could hear calling out. She never said it though. Amos stepped closer, put his hands gently on her arms and kissed her so softly that she felt certain she would melt into her shoes.

Then, without a word, he slipped his hand over hers, and they walked back to the buggy. Or rather Hope floated back.

Goose bumps indeed.

This was even better than that.

As they rode home, neither felt the need to talk. Hope had forgotten how much she loved being out in the evening, hearing the clip-clop of a horse's hooves against the pavement, smelling the new mown yards, watching the stars appear. She was almost disappointed when they pulled up in front of her house. When she didn't immediately reach for the door handle, Amos followed her gaze to the little house.

"Looks pretty different from the day we moved in," Hope admitted.

"Looks like a home."

Amos insisted on walking her to the door. He didn't kiss her again, but he squeezed her hand and whispered, "See you tomorrow."

Tomorrow's luncheon! It was an off Sunday, and Amos had invited her family to eat with his. She'd forgotten about it.

She walked into the house and then the kitchen in something of a daze. She recognized the murmur of two boys—not three. John was reading to Isaac. She opened her kitchen cabinets, wondering what she could make for the luncheon, knowing it wouldn't matter because there would be plenty of food. And besides, she could deal with it in the morning.

So, instead of interrupting her boys or worrying about Lucas, or dashing around the kitchen whipping up a cake... instead of doing any of those things, she made a hot cup of herbal tea, took it to the dining room table, and gave herself a few minutes to allow her mind to skim back over the evening.

She needed to think about how she felt. For many years, she'd avoided giving time or energy to matters of the heart. But it was possible—highly possible—that she was falling for Amos. He was kind, handsome, generous. It had been a long time since she'd felt romantically inclined. In the final few years of her marriage, what with the financial pressures and the constant struggle, she and Daniel had grown apart. She'd thought it was normal then. She'd thought it probably happened to all couples who had been married for years.

Maybe, though, it wasn't about how old you were.

Maybe it was about one heart reaching toward another.

She should have been frightened even to think about putting her heart on the line. Amos was wealthy and established. She was poor and new in town. Amos had raised five girls and all had flown the coop. She was in the midst of raising three boys. Plus, they barely knew one another. But for some reason, those things didn't scare her.

She couldn't be any more alone than she already was. Certainly she couldn't predict the future, but if things went poorly, she suspected they would still be friends. They were mature enough to know that every glimmer of affection didn't end in marriage. She should have been more wary, a certain part of her was quite aware of that. But she didn't want to be wary. She was tired of being careful and on the lookout for trouble. In fact, she was rather looking forward to seeing where—if anywhere—this would lead.

Amos couldn't decide how to broach the subject of Hope and the fact that they'd gone on a date with his family. Would they laugh? Would they remind him of his age? Would they think it a betrayal of their mother?

He didn't have to decide, and apparently, they weren't thinking any of those things. He didn't even have to bring up the subject, since it was plain by the broad smiles on their faces that they already knew.

Ada arrived first for Sunday luncheon. Her husband, Ethan, came in carrying baby Peter in one arm and a large bowl of fresh salad with strawberries, almonds and blueberries in the other.

"It's plain as can be that you're hat over suspenders for her." Ada kissed Amos on the cheek. "I'm happy for you, Dat."

Bethany was next, toting a container of peanut butter bars

he suspected were made with honey, not sugar. "We've all hoped and prayed that you would take an interest in someone."

Eunice asked if there was anything around Hope's house that she could work on. Her stepson Zeb seconded that idea with, "I'm Eunice's helper now. We can fix almost anything."

Becca hugged Amos tightly and said, "Mamm would want you to be happy," which was the first comment to bring tears to his eyes.

His sons-in-law slapped him on the back and grinned broadly, though Aaron did comment about "the matchmaker meeting his match." Even Ada rolled her eyes.

Surprisingly it was his oldest *doschder*, Sarah, who pulled him aside. "Do you want to talk about this?"

"Not much to talk about. We enjoy each other's company. We've been out to dinner once."

"And lunch several times." When he looked at her in surprise, she shrugged. "You know this town. I probably heard about your trip to Howe's before you'd finished your ice cream, and please tell me you didn't order ice cream."

"Nonfat yogurt," he assured her. But behind the teasing he saw concern, so he waited. He gave her the space to say what was on her heart.

"We're all happy for you, but please be careful."

"Careful?"

"I don't want you to get hurt."

"Ah."

"And being a stepparent, well, it has its challenges. I'm sure you've thought of that."

"I have."

"Okay," she said, and then she hugged him tightly.

Ezekiel arrived next, then Noah's parents and finally the Lambright family. Amos met Hope at her buggy. John and

Isaac and even Lucas said they'd take care of unharnessing the mare and releasing her into the pasture.

As they walked toward the picnic area, Hope smiled up at him. "Honestly, I forgot about the luncheon. I was on this date last night, and it wasn't until I stepped back into my house that I realized I needed to cook something."

"I hope you didn't stay up late worrying over it."

"Actually, I didn't. I had a cup of tea and went to bed."

"Smart move."

"Got up early and made a seven-bean salad."

"Sounds healthy."

"Yummy too."

"My *doschdern* will approve."

And then they were in the midst of the group and Ezekiel lead them in a prayer and a song. They sat at one long table that had been set up in the shade of the maple tree. It seemed to Amos that everyone was getting along swell. Young Isaac had immediately sat with Josh. John fell into easy conversation with Gideon. Lucas didn't say much, but he appeared to have a healthy enough appetite.

Everything seemed fine.

Or maybe that was what Amos wanted to see. Maybe he wasn't willing to entertain the idea that they might have bumps in their road. That's probably why he brushed off the worried looks Hope tossed her middle son. It was normal to worry about a child who was in the midst of their *rumspringa*, and if ever a teenage boy fit that picture, Lucas did.

Still, the meal passed pleasantly.

The weather was balmy but the rain held off.

And for a moment, Amos had a glimpse of what it might be like if he and Hope decided to merge their two families. Maybe it was ridiculous to entertain such thoughts so early on. Still, it felt right. At their age, what was the point in waiting? Of course, he would wait though. He needed to give Hope time to know what she wanted in her life, to know which direction she wanted to go.

After the meal, he and Hope sat in the circle of adults—swapping stories and enjoying the afternoon. The children played a game of tag then another of hide-and-seek. John joined in, though he obviously felt too old for such—twice the other children caught him hiding because he didn't fit behind the bush or under the wheelbarrow. Amos thought that Hope's oldest son was a fine young man. And Isaac acted as if he'd always been a part of their little group. Only Lucas stayed off on his own.

The afternoon was over before Amos was ready for it to be, and how long had it been since that had happened? More often than not, he was restless to get back to his porch, whatever book he was reading, his quiet time alone. He didn't want that today though. As he watched Hope's son drive their buggy down the lane, he counted the hours until he would see her again.

Which was when Gideon stepped up and said, "We need to talk."

"Sounds serious."

"Could be."

Amos nodded toward the porch, and Gideon followed him to the rockers. They could hear the women inside, soothing babies, talking softly to toddlers, laughing about some minor thing. From where they sat, Amos could see Aaron, Ethan, Noah and Zeb standing at his fence line, probably talking about horses. Or weather. Or crops. The same simple things that had taken so much of his attention for so many years.

"This is a *gut* family," Amos said. "*Gotte* has blessed me with my girls and the men they've chosen, the *grandkinner* they've given me. I have every reason to be perfectly satisfied, yet—"

He glanced at Gideon and offered a small smile. "The heart wants what the heart wants."

"I actually understand that, Amos. And I would never assume it to be my place to voice a different opinion on that matter."

"But—"

"But we need to talk about Lucas."

Somehow Amos had known this was coming. "Tell me more."

Gideon blew out a sigh, then sat forward—elbows on his knees, fingers interlaced in front of him. "He has a bad attitude, does sloppy work when he does it at all—"

"Meaning what, exactly?"

"He shows up late."

"Seems impossible, since he rides with his *mamm* and Hope is always early."

"I agree. It's odd. He also takes a longer lunch than he should and most days he leaves early."

"You've spoken to him?"

"I have."

"Should we mention the situation to Hope?"

Gideon shrugged. "What would you do if this were any other teenage boy working at the market?"

Amos didn't answer immediately. It had happened before, of course—with boys and girls. It was rare though. More often than not, if the job wasn't a good fit, the teenager quit and hired on with someone else. It was understood, in their community, in their faith, that the teenage years were a time for trying on different roles and choosing the one that felt right. That was easier for some teens more than others.

"Occasionally, I've had a one-on-one talk with the employee."

"Which I've attempted to do, with less-than-stellar results. Lucas doesn't seem to be listening. He doesn't defend himself or apologize."

"There was that time last year, where we both had to speak to the girl working in the canteen. What was her name?"

"Marsha. She was on her phone all the time." Gideon relaxed into the rocker. "I'd forgotten about her. She's working at the Blue Gate now—answering phones, if you can believe that."

They shared a small laugh.

Small, because this wasn't that.

"What's your biggest worry?" Amos asked.

"I don't want this to affect your relationship with Hope. I can see that you care for her."

"I do, and this relationship—if I were to use so bold a word—is just beginning. If we move forward, though, we will have to navigate my role with the boys as well as her role with my family."

"The former is bound to be trickier than the latter."

"Agreed."

Amos stood, and when Gideon stood as well, he pulled the young man into a hug. "*Danki*, for bringing this to me."

"Becca always reminds me to have the difficult conversation."

"Sounds like something Becca would say."

"Let me know what you want me to do."

"I will, Gideon. I'll pray on it, and we'll come up with a plan tomorrow—you, me and Hope."

"All right."

"Now, let's see if there are any of those peanut butter bars left."

Amos wasn't surprised that there was a bump in his and Hope's road. It was bound to happen. Perhaps a little sooner than he would have preferred, but sticky situations told you as much about a person as dinner dates by the lake. He only hoped that the tender young relationship they'd begun could survive whatever Lucas was able to dish out.

Chapter Eight

Amos managed to postpone the dreaded conversation until Wednesday, perhaps hoping the situation would right itself. That didn't happen. He considered himself a patient man. He'd trained many employees over the years. He'd even had to fire a few. He did not want to fire Lucas Lambright. However, the boy had once again failed to show up for his shift at the market.

Gideon looked down at the notes he'd scribbled on the pad he carried everywhere. He went over the specific problems with Lucas's work and the days those problems had occurred. As he'd said Sunday afternoon, it was something that needed to be addressed—the sooner the better.

"I can take care of this," Gideon said. "I realize you're in charge of personnel—"

"And you're in charge of operations." Amos stood and reached for his hat. "I'll handle it."

"What will you do?"

"The first goal would be to find the lad, but barring that, I need to at least speak with his *mamm*."

"I don't envy you that conversation."

"Indeed."

It was nearly thirty minutes past five, and Hope had already left for the day. Amos could have taken the buggy to her house, but the day was warm, spring was evident everywhere and he had no need to rush home. He opted to walk. It was the last day of April, and Shipshewana was showing off. Colorful flowers waved their buds everywhere he looked—in handmade baskets set outside shops, adorning window boxes and brightening yards. The grass was green, the trees resplendent as their new leaves shimmered in the slight breeze.

It was too pretty a day to ruin with this kind of conversation, but putting it off would only make things worse. Hope deserved to know.

Amos couldn't help admiring the house as he approached it. How different it looked from that first day he'd visited. Everything was neat and orderly—the yard, the porch, and no doubt the inside of the home. He knocked tentatively, then more loudly.

"I've got it, Mamm." Isaac appeared at the door, a smile wreathing his face. "Amos. *Gut* to see you."

The boy opened the door and threw his arms around Amos's waist, giving him an unembarrassed and exuberant hug. "I've been giving Oreo one peppermint a day. Not more, because Mamm said it would be bad for her teeth. And John lets me help brush her each evening. It's one of my chores."

Hope appeared in the doorway. "Isaac, let Amos come inside."

He stepped into the living room and marveled at the difference. It was still small, but it was freshly painted with a gently used couch, a rocker and an older recliner. A small bookcase against one wall held books and board games.

"This is a pleasant surprise," Hope said. "Would you like a cup of coffee or tea?"

Their eyes met then, and Amos thought they were both

remembering the last time he'd visited her home on his own, when she'd offered what she didn't have.

"Hot tea would be nice. I'm here to speak with you about a situation. Alone, may be *gut*."

"I know what that means," Isaac said cheerfully. "Something about big ears and little pitchers. I'll just pop over and visit Oreo."

"That horse has been a godsend," Hope said. "Being the youngest can be lonely, but Isaac can't seem to spend enough time with Oreo."

She pointed him toward the dining nook while she set the teakettle on the stove, popped two tea bags into two mugs and pulled out a plate of cookies. Amos watched her do those things, still thinking of the day he first met her. The difference in her demeanor and the added bounce in her step were truly amazing. Of course, he saw those same traits every day in the office, but seeing them here, in this small home, drove the point home to his heart. If you gave someone hope, they usually rose to the possibilities. Hope Lambright was a remarkable woman.

He turned back toward the nook area and let out a whistle. "I didn't realize you were a seamstress."

"I work faster when I have a treadle machine, and I did not say that so you'd find one and bring it over. Actually, to be truthful, I enjoy hand sewing. It's more relaxing."

Squares of denim and colorful cotton fabric were stacked neatly on one side of the table. On the floor were the remnants of blue jeans, housedresses, even curtains that she'd cut into usable pieces.

"It's amazing what people get rid of," Hope added. "Most of that I found at a garage sale and some at the thrift store in town."

"This is beautiful work, Hope. How in the world do you find the time?"

"My boys don't require that much supervision, and you know what they say about idle hands…"

"Well, yours have not been idle." He picked up what looked like a diaper bag, a charming patchwork of denim and flowered cotton. She'd made smaller bags, blankets, book bags, even baby slings. "Where will you sell these?"

"When I have an adequate supply made, I thought I'd approach some of the stores."

"I'd be happy to carry them at the market. We have a gift shop next to the canteen. Or you could have a vendor stall."

Hope cocked her head, seemed to give the idea careful consideration, then nodded. "*Danki*. The gift shop would be preferable. That way I wouldn't need to man the booth."

"It's a deal then."

She cleared a spot on the table and brought over the two mugs of tea. Amos picked up the platter of cookies—peanut butter if he wasn't mistaken.

Once they were settled at the table, Hope jumped right in. "From the expression on your face, I gather this is bad news."

"It is. Lucas didn't show up for work again today."

"Again?"

"He didn't show up yesterday, either."

"He certainly rode to work with me both days. Where could he be going so early in the morning? And why?" She let out a sigh and sipped her hot tea. "I suspect you have more to say. May as well tell me all of it."

Amos was amazed she was taking the news so well, but then it couldn't have been a surprise. On the first day he'd met her, she'd indicated that Lucas would be a difficult employee.

"When he is there, his work ethic leaves a lot to be desired. Mostly he…avoids his responsibilities."

"I wish I could say I'm surprised, but I did warn you."

"*Ya*, you did." Amos bought himself some time by sipping his tea and reaching for a cookie. Peanut butter was one of his favorites. With his *doschdern* watching his weight so closely, he rarely had them. Instead of eating the cookie, though, he set it on a napkin, gathered his courage and looked at Hope.

"I don't think the market is a *gut* fit for Lucas." He pulled a piece of paper from his pocket and set it on the table between them. "I've made a list of a few places in town that he may apply for work at. Two are Amish and two are *Englisch*. All four are *gut* employers."

And there, in a blink of an eye, her demeanor changed. She stared at him in disbelief, stood, sat again, and shook her head. "You're firing him?"

"I don't have a choice."

"Of course you have a choice. No one's telling you what to do. You're the owner."

"I am, but I have to do what's best for the market."

"So, that's it? You don't even give him a second chance?"

"I've given him a second, a third, even a fourth chance." Amos could tell that Hope was becoming angry and defensive. He even understood why, but that didn't mean he could give in to her motherly reaction. He had a business to run. He tried being more specific. "Lucas is insolent and lazy. He's also dangerous to have around."

"Dangerous?" Two bright spots of color now stained Hope's cheeks, and sparks were flying from her eyes. "He's only fifteen years old. I fail to see how he can be dangerous, unless you consider not showing up to clean out a horse stall hazardous to your market."

"He was smoking in the barn, Hope. Right next to the hay

bales. I can't have that. He put my animals at risk. He put the entire market at risk."

She stood, arms crossed, a scowl etched across her face. "I see you've made your decision. I appreciate your coming by to tell me face-to-face, though it would have been nice if you'd offered Lucas the same courtesy."

"I'd be glad to if I could find him." Amos stood, too, understanding that she wanted him to leave. This wasn't going at all like he'd hoped. But really, how else could it have gone? "I know these things are difficult to hear—"

"Do you? One of your girls was fired from her job?"

"Yes, actually. More than once." He almost laughed thinking of how many jobs Ada had been through before she'd found her real passion—saving animals. Maybe that was what Lucas was missing. Maybe he needed help finding his passion. "Perhaps you could have Lucas meet with Ezekiel."

"Counseling sessions. That's what you're suggesting. Lucas won't do that. We tried it in Lancaster."

"I see."

"He needs a father figure, Amos. He needs someone who won't give up on him."

Ouch. Was that what he'd done? He didn't know how to answer her. Didn't know what he could or should say to this woman to ease her pain. So, instead of digging the hole he was standing in even deeper, he wished her a *gut* afternoon and left the peanut butter cookie and cup of tea on the table. Walking back to the market, the day looked less pristine, less full of possibility.

Had he given up on Lucas?

Had Hope been suggesting that he be a father figure to her son?

How would he even do that?

And what did this mean for their relationship? Was it destined to end even before it had properly begun?

He didn't have any answers. He was sixty years old, and some days it felt as if he was still figuring life out. Or trying to. He didn't know the best way to help Lucas, but the one thing he knew for certain was that he couldn't abide the look of devastation on Hope's face. He'd find a way to help her, even if it meant mentoring her insolent teenager.

After all, how hard could it be?

He'd raised five girls on his own. Certainly he could handle one angry boy. But he'd need to keep a rein on his feelings for Hope until they had this part figured out. And yes—he could admit to himself that he was developing feelings for her. What single man wouldn't? She was beautiful, kind, hardworking…

He lost the trail of his thoughts while adding adjectives to his description of Hope. Then the market came into view. He was the owner of that market. A sixty-year-old man who had lived and worked in this town nearly all of his life at one place. The market.

He once again considered the age difference between himself and Hope. Fourteen years was a lot. Fourteen years might be too big a gap to bridge. In that moment, staring at the market that had grown beyond his wildest dreams, a heavy dread settled over him. He'd been foolish to believe they might fall in love. He'd even envisioned the boys living at his home. The buggy had careened off in front of the proverbial horse. He hadn't thought it through. Hadn't considered all the details. Hadn't dealt with the question of Lucas.

Why had he asked her on a date?

Why had he kissed her?

Nein. He wasn't what Hope or her family needed.

He'd never in all his years of being a widower felt attracted to another woman. Why now? Perhaps it was this nagging sense of not being needed anymore. If that was the case, he could volunteer somewhere.

Or mentor a local teen.

The one certainty was that he would need to do what was best for the market. It was his life's work. It was his children's legacy. He couldn't let an irresponsible teenager threaten that. Could he? Perhaps there was another way. Maybe he could let Lucas shadow him. There were tasks that needed to be done, and Amos would be there to see that they were done correctly.

Mentor the boy.

Stay an appropriate distance from the mother.

Keep his feelings out of things.

The question was whether he'd be able to do all three equally well. Because if he couldn't, one of them was bound to experience a bit of heartbreak.

Hope was heartsick—literally.

She felt slightly nauseous. Her worst nightmare was happening all over again. All the things that had gone wrong in Lancaster were going wrong here. How had she thought that a change in location would fix whatever ailed her middle son?

That evening, she did her best to keep a smile plastered on her face. She might have succeeded in fooling Isaac, but John knew something was up. He suggested she go see Oreo while he oversaw his younger brother's bath. Turning away quickly to hide her tears, she fled the house.

Was this her fault?

Maybe she shouldn't have taken a job. Maybe she should have stayed home to watch over her middle son. Only how would that have helped? He was supposed to be at work, at the same place she worked. Her mind played over the last few weeks, the lame reasons he'd given her for not being able to take Isaac home when he left the market. In truth, he'd been leaving the market as soon as they arrived. At one point Lucas had looked her in the eyes and told her he was leaving early to see about a way to make extra money— a Saturday job. And she had believed him!

She walked up to the pasture fence. The black-and-white mare trotted over to where she stood, reaching her big head over the fence to sniff for a treat. "Sorry, girl. I didn't bring anything."

The horse forgave her, allowing Hope to scratch her neck, breathe in the scent of her and even cry into her coat. As darkness fell and she heard the crickets begin to chirp, Hope realized that she had been a fool.

She'd believed her son was doing better because she wanted with all of her heart for that to be true.

She'd also believed that Amos might be the one for her. "Foolish," she whispered to the mare, who tossed her head once, then moved away to graze on new sprouts of grass.

Amos was a good man. She didn't doubt that for a minute. But he wasn't *the one* for her. How could he be? Anyone who cared for her would have to care for her children too. Wasn't that how marriage worked? And although she thought that he did have feelings for her—she'd seen it in his eyes that night they'd walked around Lake Shipshewana—she didn't think he had it in him to help raise a rebellious teen.

Help raise her teen.

She'd really let her imagination run out of the horse stall, hadn't she? No more. She dried her tears and promised herself no more foolishness. She was a single *mamm* who was responsible for three young men. That was her purpose, and if it was hard sometimes then so be it.

By the time she walked back into the house, Isaac was ready for bed.

"I can read him his story," John offered.

"You've done plenty. *Danki*." When she went into the boys' room, Isaac was watching her closely. He scooched over so she could sit on his bed. "Care for a story?"

"I guess. Maybe. What's wrong, Mamm? Is it Lucas? Are we going to have to move again?"

She closed her eyes for a moment, mainly so he wouldn't see the tears shining there. But when had she started hiding her feelings from her boys? So she opened her eyes, let the tears fall and wiped them away. He launched himself into her arms and gave her a hug big enough to nearly topple her over.

"I am worried about Lucas," she admitted.

"Because he disappears with those rough kids?"

Good grief, even ten-year-old Isaac had seen the things she'd ignored. "That does worry me, yes. Though we're called to love rough-looking kids like everyone else."

"Oh. Is it the cigarettes? I told him it smells bad."

"That too, but Isaac..." She patted the bed so that Isaac would lie down again. "Lucas is struggling, same as we all do at times."

"I struggled when my teacher sent Hoppy home with Mary Beth last weekend. I was sure she'd pick me."

"And she will pick you, soon enough. But yes, it is a little like that." They spent the next ten minutes talking about *rum-springa*, that running around time when teens were allowed to try things from the *Englisch* way of life. Then she read him a short passage from his library book, and he promised to go to sleep. The room was small with three twin beds in it, but it looked homey. It looked good. She hadn't made a mistake moving to Shipshewana. Her only mistake had been in believing it would solve all of their problems.

When she walked back into the kitchen, John was waiting for her. They each had hot tea and peanut butter cookies. The cookies reminded her of Amos and how he'd smiled at the sight of the platter of sweets. She'd even made them with applesauce so he could eat them without betraying his healthy eating pledge.

"What will we do now?" John asked.

It was a simple, direct question, and she answered it as honestly as she could. They wouldn't ignore Lucas's misdeeds any longer. They would intercede in an appropriate way. They would find steps to help him through this difficult time.

"Don't let him take advantage of you, Mamm."

"I won't."

"I love him, but I don't understand him."

"Same."

"Do you think Amos will fire him tomorrow?"

"If he bothers to show up for work, yes. I believe he will." She straightened her posture and pushed away the hurt that threatened to consume her. Now that she'd had a few hours to move through the cycles of grief, she realized that she'd overreacted when Amos had tried to break the news. She'd blamed the messenger instead of the person who'd actually done those things. "Amos has every right to fire your *bruder*. Lucas must learn there are consequences to his actions."

"Where will he find another job?"

The small piece of paper with the list of businesses still lay there on the table. She showed it to John. He pointed out the two establishments he thought would be best, and she nodded.

"Think I'll turn in myself," he said. "I love my job, but it wears me out."

"Good night, son."

Kissing her on top of the head, he murmured, "It's going to be okay," which made her feel like a child.

She tried to stay awake and wait up for Lucas. She wanted to do this now. To get it over with. She read her Bible, then attempted to stitch the border on a baby bib, but her eyes were simply too tired. Finally, she made sure the porch light was on and the door was unlocked.

Hope didn't think she'd sleep.

She did. In fact, she fell into a deep, dreamless slumber almost immediately. Perhaps because the worst had happened and she could stop dreading it. Her final thought before drifting off was that they might be back in the same situation that had caused them to leave Lancaster, but their situation was most certainly different.

This was a *gut*, small community.

Amos was a *gut* friend.

Ezekiel was a kind bishop.

She would see him the next day. She'd seek his council. She'd do whatever she needed to in order to save her son.

Chapter Nine

A small part of Amos worried that Hope wouldn't come into work the next day. He should have known her better than that. She'd never been even a minute late.

She smiled tightly when he walked in, then pretended to be busy thumbing through a stack of papers. At least he thought she was pretending. He was surprised she even had a stack of papers. The office was in great shape. Everything was filed, mailed, copied to department heads. She had done her job well, and he realized in that moment that he should recommend her placement in the office become permanent. He'd speak to Gideon about it.

But first they needed to deal with the problem at hand.

He could call her into his office where their conversation would be more private, but he didn't want to further alarm her. So, instead, he went out and motioned toward the chair positioned beside her tidy desk. "May I?"

"Of course."

"First, I want to apologize."

Her eyebrows shot up, but she didn't interrupt.

"I'm afraid I came across somewhat cold and callous yesterday, and that is not what I meant to communicate."

"Okay."

"I do still believe that Lucas's current position is not a good match for him."

Her posture, which had relaxed a fraction, stiffened.

"I also spent a good amount of time last night thinking about what you said, Hope. I agree that Lucas needs a mentor. Now, I'm not sure I'm the right person for that, but I'd be willing to try if you'd like me to."

"You would?"

It tore at his heart that she looked so surprised, but then she didn't really know him. She didn't know how patiently he'd raised his *doschdern*, and she was no doubt used to people harshly judging Lucas. Whether he'd done that or not, he wasn't sure, but Amos did understand a cry for help when he heard one. This woman was desperate for help with her son. And perhaps, in some harder to understand way, Lucas was also asking for help with his behavior.

"Did Lucas come to work with you today?"

Her chin rose. "Yes. I spoke with him this morning. I told him until he was fired by you or Gideon then he would continue showing up for his assigned job."

She blinked twice, then looked away. "I spoke to him of actions and consequences. I'm not sure I got through though. I never know, with Lucas, if I am getting through or not."

"Okay. What do you say that we talk to him?"

"Now?"

"Yes. Now. But first, let me tell you what I have in mind."

After he was certain she understood the parameters of what he was suggesting, they searched for Lucas. They found him in the barn, mucking out a horse stall, the customary frown on his face.

"Guess you're here to fire me." Lucas leaned the tool against the stall wall, crossed his arms and shrugged. "Never much liked this job anyway."

"You will be respectful to Amos, son. With your words and your manner."

"Okay. Whatever that means."

"It means you give me the courtesy of looking at me when we're having a conversation." The words came out a bit more gruffly than he'd intended. What was it about this boy that pushed all Amos's buttons? He pulled in a deep breath and tried again. "It is true that this job is not a good fit for you—apparently you agree with that as strongly as your *mamm* and I do."

Lucas finally had caught on to the fact that something different than what he expected was happening here. His gaze flitted from his mother to Amos, back and forth, as if he were trying to figure out what was coming next and how to prepare for it. How did a fifteen-year-old become that defensive?

"Your *mamm* believes you need a mentor."

"A mentor? What is that supposed to do for me?"

"Well, if you have questions, you can ask them. If you're unsure how to respond to a situation, you can check. A mentor would try to provide support for you vocationally, emotionally and spiritually."

Slow dawning crossed Lucas's face. "You? You're going to mentor me?"

"I've agreed to try. If you're willing to do the same."

"And I'd, like…get paid for that?"

Amos had spent quite a bit of time this morning thinking on that question. "*Nein*. You wouldn't."

Lucas put his hands on his hips and stared at the ground, shaking his head.

"You wouldn't get paid for shadowing me," Amos added. "But once I'm able to trust you with tasks to complete, then you would receive the same compensation you do now."

"Free labor, in other words, until I 'prove myself.'" He put finger quotes around the last two words.

Before Amos could answer, Hope jumped in.

"You are fortunate that Amos is offering to do this. He's a busy man with a huge business and a large family. He owes you—" She fisted her hands at her side, the scowl on her face growing even more pronounced. "He owes us nothing. If you want to walk up and down the streets of Shipshewana looking for a job that will pay less than you're making now, be my guest. But make no mistake. The shenanigans of the last few weeks are over."

Amos wanted to shout, "Go, Hope!" He didn't. He ran a thumb under his suspenders and waited for the boy to answer.

"Fine. I guess."

"That won't do, I'm afraid." Amos had decided to be firm on this point. He wouldn't take a lukewarm agreement from the boy. "You have to commit to this, Lucas. It's your decision, not mine or your mother's."

They'd finally caught him by surprise.

"Can I have time to think about it?"

"Absolutely." Amos held out a hand for the pitchfork Lucas had been using to clean the hay in the barn. "I'll take that. You're done here."

Lucas thrust the farm tool at him, slipped his hands into his pockets and walked away.

"I'm so sorry, Amos…"

"No need for that." He stored the tool in its proper place, then motioned toward the main office building. Going back to work wasn't what his heart was urging him to do. He wanted to invite Hope for a stroll, for coffee, for a pretzel from JoJo's. He wanted to spend time with her and try to salvage their relationship. He wanted to tell her how proud he was that she'd been firm with her son.

He didn't do any of those things. He'd convinced himself the night before that he needed to be supportive but keep his distance. Hope deserved someone perfect for her. Maybe someone with children her boys' ages. Definitely not someone with grandchildren.

"He's rude and insolent," Hope said. "I see now that I've let it go too far."

"He's fifteen. Most teens grow out of it."

"But will Lucas?"

The woebegone look on her face caused Amos's stomach to twist. He longed to pull her into his arms. Instead, he reached for her hand, squeezed it, then let it go. "We'll pray, and we'll help him any way we can."

They walked back toward the office. At the outer door, Amos made an excuse for not going inside with her. He needed space, fresh air, some time alone. He stayed away until it was after lunch, then sequestered himself in his office answering phone calls and dealing with managerial tasks. When he heard her soft "Good night," he let out a sigh of relief. Maybe he could focus with her gone.

But he couldn't.

He kept seeing the worry on her brow, the sadness in her eyes, the love for a child that she didn't know how to help.

A soft tapping on his doorframe twenty minutes later pulled him from his reverie. Lucas stood there, slightly less defiant, his expression worried—like his mother's.

"What can I do for you, Lucas?"

"I accept your offer."

"Wunderbaar." Amos had written up a simple list outlining the mentor/mentee relationship. He pushed it across the desk.

Lucas walked toward the desk, picked up the sheet of paper and stood staring at it for a moment.

"You're welcome to sit."

Lucas gave a quick shake of his head as he studied the sheet. Amos remembered every line he'd written there. He'd decided to keep it simple and to the point.

Arrive on time, every day.
Stay until workday is over.
Speak with respect to others.
Follow the rules of the market, which include no smoking or drinking on the grounds.
Ask for help if you need it.

Finally the boy—and that was what Lucas was, just a boy trying to find his way—looked up. His next words surprised Amos.

"Why are you doing this?"

It was a serious question that deserved a serious answer. "Because I would want to be helped if I were in your situation."

Lucas nodded, stared at the sheet of rules one last time, then accepted the pen that Amos offered and signed his name on the bottom. When he pushed the sheet of paper back across the desk, Amos shook his head. "Your copy. Keep it."

"Right." He folded the sheet, being careful to match up the edges, and stuck it in his pocket. "When do we start?"

Amos had purposely set the boy's start time an hour before Hope's start time. Lucas needed to step out of his mother's wing. He needed to learn to be responsible, and that would start with him getting up early and getting to work on time—by himself. "Tomorrow morning. Eight o'clock sharp."

Lucas nodded, and without another word, he walked away.

In that moment, Amos was somehow able to see past the insolent teenager to the hurting young man beneath. A young man who had lost his father, who had found his father—dead—in the family barn, who was struggling to decide who or what he wanted to be.

Amos closed his eyes and vowed to remember that insight.

He had no illusion that the days ahead would be easy.

He prayed that he was the man for the job.

He hoped that things would turn out well—not just for Lucas, but also for the entire family. He still believed that his daydream of having a romantic relationship with Hope was just that—a daydream. He wouldn't indulge it going forward. Instead, he would find a way to be content with the life he had. He'd need to accept that he wasn't meant to love again. Those days, it would seem, were destined to remain in his past.

Hope wasn't sure how to deal with her frustration regarding Lucas, so she did what she had often done: She spent the next week working longer hours, attempting to pour the restless energy building inside her into something positive. Her supply of handsewn items grew, and she wondered if she should take them into the office. Amos had offered. Had that been out of pity? Out of duty? Or because he thought what she'd created was genuinely good?

Fortunately, she didn't have to worry about that for long. Sarah, Amos's oldest *doschder*, stopped by for a visit on Saturday morning.

"I hope I'm not intruding."

"Not at all." Hope led her into the kitchen, which was full of bright sunshine and looked rather like a seamstress's shop.

"Wow." Sarah handed over Grace and walked closer to the work area Hope had set up on the kitchen table. "You did all of this?"

"*Ya*. It's just something I…play with."

"Play? Don't sell yourself short, Hope. This is *gut* craftsmanship." She held up one of the baby bibs and a matching set of burp towels. They were denim on one side, cotton fabric printed with pink bunnies on the other. "This is adorable. Can I buy it?"

"*Nein*. It's yours if you want it."

"No way. Nope. I'll only take it if you let me pay. What are you going to do with all this stuff?"

Hope explained that Amos had offered to sell it in the canteen. "I'm not sure how to price things though."

Sarah turned toward her with a bright smile. "If you have hot tea and something sweet to eat, we can have a business planning session."

They had the session in the backyard. Hope had come home from the market one day to find a newly painted picnic table and benches behind her house. "I need to ask Ezekiel who left it, so I can thank them properly," she explained to Sarah.

"He won't tell you. He probably doesn't even know. It's just the way we do things in Shipshewana. Someone has something someone else needs, so they deliver it. If you decide you don't want the item, you pass it on to someone else."

"You know, Sarah…" Hope was still holding Grace, who was precious and beautiful. The darling child sucked her fingers and stared up at Hope with wide, curious, trusting eyes. "Not every town operates the way Shipshewana does. Not every Amish community is as generous."

"I suppose that's true, but Shipshewana isn't perfect. We have our problems, same as anyone else."

"Such as…?" Hope wasn't asking out of idle curiosity. She was beginning to wonder if she'd fallen into paradise, which was a problem because she didn't believe paradise existed—not this side of heaven anyway. If it seemed like a perfect, flawless place then she wasn't seeing things clearly, and it was important that she did so.

"Drinking problems. Marital problems that need to be addressed more openly instead of pushed aside. Teenage pregnancy and underage drinking. The *Englisch* here…" She stared at the backyard then shook her head. "We've learned to live well side by side, but they don't understand our leniency toward *youngies*."

"You mean during their *rumspringa*."

"Exactly. In the eyes of the church, or of their family, it's okay for them to try *Englisch* things, but that doesn't mean it's legal."

"Give me an example."

"Driving, before they're of legal age to do so and without an official license."

"Yes, I can see how that would be a problem. What else?"

"Alcohol, of course, before the legal age. But also drugs." She told Hope about how her husband had struggled with drugs, that he'd spent time in an Illinois prison, that it had taken years for him to see himself worthy of forgiveness and a second chance.

"I had no idea."

"Noah is a new man. He's changed. His time in prison changed him. Now he's home, and he's grateful to have the opportunity to start his life over." Sarah accepted a fussing Grace and proceeded to feed her. "Noah and I work with youth in the area who are struggling with alcohol or drugs."

Hope stiffened.

Had Amos mentioned Lucas's problems to his family? But he didn't know about the trouble with alcohol Lucas had in Lancaster, and as far as Hope knew Lucas had not started drinking again here in Shipshewana.

"You're thinking of something," Sarah said softly. "Care to share?"

Any other time, she might not have. But Hope needed a friend, and she knew that the only way to have a true friendship was to be honest with one another. So she told Sarah about Lucas's problems in Lancaster, about being arrested, how their local church and bishop had become involved.

"How did that go?"

"Not well, to be honest. Lucas didn't understand how he'd done anything else that a dozen other *youngies* hadn't also done. He considered himself unlucky to have been caught, but he didn't see a need for reprisal or restitution. The bishop assigned Lucas to a charity work crew, but that didn't go well either. Lucas was resentful and the deacon in charge of the work crew was quite strict." Hope hesitated, then added, "It's not the only reason we left Pennsylvania, but it was one reason."

Sarah's response surprised her. "That's a lot for you to carry, Hope."

"Well. I'm his *mamm*."

"Of course, but what I mean is that's a heavy burden for you to shoulder alone. My husband's parents had each other, and still those years while Noah was away took their toll."

Hope shrugged. What could she say? She was in this alone. That was just a fact of her life.

"You know, often the people who come to our meetings are not the teens themselves, but rather the teens' families."

"Why would they come to a meeting?"

"To support each other. Sometimes what one family has tried might work for another. Sometimes it's just nice to know you're not the only one struggling with a particular problem."

"I guess that makes sense."

"Will you think about coming?" Sarah picked up the pen and wrote on the sheet of paper next to where they'd been listing prices. She put the date and location of the next three meetings. "Come with or without Lucas. You may find it helps."

"I'll think about it."

At that moment Isaac dashed into the yard. He'd been playing with the *Englisch* neighbor a few doors down, and they both skidded to a stop. Hope reminded them there were fresh oatmeal cookies in the house and hollered after them, "Only two each."

She and Sarah spent the next half hour going over prices for her sewing goods.

Sarah gave her ideas for bundling things together and offering a discount. "You could also have a different special each week, with a twenty percent discount. Rotate through your stock. And have a quarterly Clean the Bins Sale with deeper discounts. That way you'll always have space for new items, and often people who stop for a sale will end up buying other things at full price."

"You have a real knack for this," she told Sarah.

"I'm Amos's *doschder*. I practically grew up in that market. Some of it was bound to rub off on me."

She didn't want to let her hopes rise, but the money could help—a lot. Her job at the market was only guaranteed until July 1. She'd run the numbers a dozen times. She couldn't make enough in the intervening weeks to keep the household running, prepare for winter and send money to Edwin Bing. But if she could sell her homemade goods, it might be enough.

Hope walked Sarah to the buggy parked out front, held Grace as Sarah climbed up into the buggy and with some reluctance handed the sweet baby over. "Anytime you need a sitter, please let me know. I'd love to spend a few hours rocking your *boppli*."

"*Danki*, Hope. I may take you up on that."

"By the way, why did you stop by today? It couldn't have been to help me with my pricing. You didn't even know about it."

"Just to say hi."

Sarah smiled. The simple, genuine gesture lifted Hope's mood a bit.

"I'm glad you did," Hope said.

"Living in a new town can be hard. I want you to know that we care about you, and we're glad you and your family are here."

Which were words that Hope sorely needed to hear.

As Sarah drove away, Hope realized that her life wasn't all about Lucas and his problems. Isaac was in the kitchen this moment, enjoying a snack with his new friend. John was at work, earning extra money, and he'd found the courage to ask one of the girls from their church community out on a date. Sarah enjoyed both her job at the market and her hobby repurposing old things into items that looked new and beautiful.

Spending time with Sarah led Hope's thoughts back to Amos. She could imagine what it would be like to be a part of such a large, caring, energetic family. It would be a different kind of existence. To have that big of a support network was something she'd never experienced.

It hadn't escaped her notice that Amos had not asked her out on another date. She could stew over that or she could ask him why. Or she could give it some time. Life was good and full of blessings, even if she was destined to pass through it alone. Worrying over that changed nothing. Her hours would be better spent earning and saving money for winter—a time of year when there always seemed to be extra expenses.

Her social needs could wait.

But she wouldn't deny the sadness that she felt.

She had hoped that maybe Amos was the one for her.

She'd hoped that he felt about her the same way that she felt about him.

Chapter Ten

The next week Amos spent preparing for the larger-than-normal Memorial Day crowds. Most weeks their vendor section was only open on Tuesdays and Wednesdays. For the Memorial Day weekend, the market also opened on Monday. It didn't sound like something that would take a lot of extra work and planning, but it did.

As for his mentoring, Amos thought the last two and a half weeks had gone fairly well. As promised, Lucas had appeared at his door at 8:00 a.m. sharp. He hadn't had much to say, but he'd been there, on time, and he seemed at least marginally interested in what they had to do. The holiday meant that they would need to make space for extra vendors. That required coordinating things between the front office—Hope—vendors and the general manager, Gideon. Temporary structures were set up to house an extra row, and Amos oversaw the placement of those booths, as well as assigning them to vendors.

"Thirty additional vendors. Thirty additional booths. What's there to do?" Lucas seemed perplexed.

"Sounds simple enough," Amos admitted. "But it takes a little finessing."

"Huh?"

"You don't want to put competing products right next to each other."

Lucas shook his head.

Amos ran his fingers through his beard, staring back toward his office. A month ago, he'd spent his midmorning time sharing a coffee break with Hope. Not any longer. He'd made good on two promises to himself: he'd mentor Lucas to the best of his abilities and give Hope the space to find someone closer to her age—someone who would have the time and energy to raise three growing boys.

Mentoring Lucas had been surprisingly rewarding. That said, many days, like today, the boy seemed clueless as to what was being asked of him. Which was fine. There were things he couldn't know yet. Amos didn't mind explaining the what, where, when or even why of running a market. On days that Lucas was open to learning, things went well. On days he was closed down, things went poorly. Amos hadn't yet determined what provoked one attitude over the other. He was still learning.

Amos motioned toward a bench in the shade.

Isaac shrugged and followed him there.

"Your mom is bringing her sewing things in to the canteen this week. Right?"

"*Ya.* I heard her say as much. She even had me and Isaac carry some boxes out to the buggy for her."

"Great. So we wouldn't want to put your *mamm*'s beautiful handiwork right next to someone else who is selling the same thing. Not that I have someone else selling the same thing, but let's say I did."

"Okay. We don't put two vendors selling similar products together. Why not?"

"Instead, we would put one person at this end of the vendor booths and the other person at the opposite end. That way people who start on one end and then tucker out still have a chance to see and purchase those products. The two booths would complement each other instead of compete with each other."

"Makes sense."

"We wouldn't want to position food booths right next to fragrance booth—candles, perfumes, that sort of thing."

"Okay."

"We have a guy who does chainsaw art, and he likes to demonstrate how he creates his pieces. He's so loud, we put him as far away from everyone as possible while still allowing him to be in the flow of traffic."

Lucas seemed to be paying attention. He even appeared to be marginally interested when it was just the two of them. As soon as other people became involved—vendors, market employees or folks bringing things in to be auctioned—his attention fled. He'd back off and direct his gaze in the opposite direction. A few times, Amos caught him staring at his hands. Was he wishing he had a phone to look at? What was really happening here?

Overall though, the days went well.

Amos had high hopes that perhaps time and patience would make a good employee out of Lucas—maybe not at the market, but if he learned to pay attention and follow instructions, if he focused on being dependable, then he could work anywhere.

He'd sent the lad off for an hour lunch break and made his way into the canteen area, when he nearly collided with Hope.

"Amos!"

"Hope."

"Didn't realize you'd be in here."

"Searching for some lunch," he said. "I'm a bit late though."

"Oh."

"Care to join me?"

She cocked her head as if considering it. "Can't. My boss gives me an hour for lunch and I've already used most of it setting up my craft display."

"Show me."

Her knack at decorating a small space was almost as grand as her skill at sewing.

"I love how you did this where they exit," he said.

"Do you know why?"

"Well, being a bit of a marketer myself…" Amos couldn't help wriggling his eyebrows at his play on words. It earned him a small laugh from Hope so he considered it a success. "I'd say that you don't want to put it where they come in be-cause—"

"They're starving when they come in."

"And tired."

"Exactly."

"But when they leave, they'll be in the mood to shop again." Amos turned and studied the nearly empty canteen. The next day week it would be stuffed with people. Memorial Day crowds were always among their largest.

"I thought they could choose their merchandise and take it back to the cashier. I was going to make a sign with those instructions. If that's okay with you."

"Sounds perfect. I'll speak with the canteen manager to let them know to expect buyers and how to code it to your account."

"It won't be too much extra work for them?"

He'd noticed that about Hope. She nearly always thought about how a thing would affect other people. "*Nein*. Not at all."

"Great." She turned, as if ready to leave.

"There is one thing though." He waited until she turned back toward him, worried, wondering what she'd missed. "You may sell out next week."

"Sell out?"

"*Ya*. I've seen it happen."

"Huh."

"I'm not saying that so you'll go home and work more hours."

"Course not."

"Just wanted you to be aware of the possibility—in case you have any extra stock at home."

"Thank you, Amos."

Over the years, he'd become adept at reading people. He could tell that Hope wanted to ask him about how her son had been doing and whether he regretted the mentorship. She didn't, and he was glad. It was too early. They needed to give Lucas breathing room and a chance to make decisions about his life.

The question was what Luke would do with those things. Would he use them to help his situation? Or would he sabotage a good thing? He thought they would know soon enough.

Hope gave a little wave and walked back toward the office. She was a *gut* person—a *wunderbaar mamm* and a hardworking employee. Not to mention she was kind and beautiful. There was little wonder why he'd begun to fall for her.

He'd worked that out of his system though.

He'd come to his senses.

Now all he had to do was wait for his brain to send the message to his heart.

The week after Hope bumped into Amos in the canteen started off well, then headed steadily and surely downhill.

Monday night, her plumbing sprung a leak. As water spilled out from beneath the kitchen sink, John rushed to turn it off at the gadget near the street.

"How did you know how to do that?" Hope asked.

"Amos showed me."

"Amos? When was he—"

"On the workday."

"Ah."

Together they tried to fix the leak, but they didn't seem to have the tools or the expertise.

John banged around under the sink for more than an hour. The last time she'd hollered to Isaac to turn the water back on, it had soaked him, Hope and the kitchen floor. Finally, he backed out from under the sink and stood, craning his neck to the left and right and rubbing at his shoulder. "Want me to call Amos?"

"*Nein.* I'll just phone a plumber."

Which ended up costing her 168 dollars, and made her worry that her pride had caused her to waste some of their limited savings. Certainly Amos would have known how to fix the doohickey that had broken, but she had the strange sensation that she was once again on her own. She couldn't pinpoint why she felt that way, but over the years she'd learned to trust her instincts.

He didn't exactly avoid her at work, but nearly so.

He wasn't rude, but neither did he relax in her presence.

Amos was sending all the signals that equaled *not interested.*

Hence the plumber and the bill, which she paid for from their cash jar kept on hand for treats or emergencies. It wasn't a proper savings account, but it was the best she could do at the moment.

On Tuesday the crowds at the market were huge—larger

even than the day before, which she hadn't thought possible. She'd seen them steadily grow as the May weather became warmer and even more pleasant, but she was still surprised to see cars stretched down the road, waiting to be allowed into the parking area. She barely saw Amos or Lucas on Tuesday. They were spending their time out on the grounds, tending to emergencies. When she asked Lucas if he liked the work better than what he did before, he shrugged and averted his gaze to his plate.

Then Tuesday evening, Isaac came home with the thrilling announcement that he had been chosen to take care of Hoppy for the first month of summer. "My teacher says not to worry about feed and such. They provide it. And there's a hutch to keep him in too, but..." He stood on first his left foot and then his right, his eyes locked on the ceiling as his right hand tugged on his earlobe.

"What is it, son? Look at me and tell me what you're worried about."

Isaac did as requested and attempted a small smile. "Not exactly sure how we'll get the hutch home is all. Not sure it will fit in the buggy. Plus, we don't usually take the buggy to school—it being so close and all."

She most certainly would take the buggy if it was the only way to bring Hoppy and his habitat home. Based on Isaac's description, that didn't seem likely.

"It's huge. Easily this big, and it sets on a kind of table." He stretched his arms as wide as possible to demonstrate *huge*.

Didn't sound like it would fit in her buggy. It might fit in a newer buggy that had a larger back seat area.

Again she thought of asking Amos for help.

But really, it seemed silly. She was an independent woman. She'd managed just fine before she'd met Amos Yoder. She hadn't depended on help from a man when they'd lived in Lancaster. "We'll figure something out," she assured him.

After dinner, she spotted her neighbor Milly out watering their plants. A nice *Englisch* woman with gray hair bobbed short and a passel of grandchildren, she beamed on seeing Hope.

They chatted about the weather, the yards and the children before Hope gathered her nerve.

"I was wondering if we could borrow the wagon I see your grandchildren playing with." Hope explained about her son and Hoppy.

"Will it fit in a wagon?"

"Not sure. If it doesn't fit in it, we could probably balance it on top."

"No problem," Milly said. "You can take it with you tonight and bring it back when you're done."

Lucas had been quiet but still fairly easy to get along with since starting his apprenticeship with Amos, but on Wednesday he woke in a foul mood that he couldn't or wouldn't explain. She thought it might have something to do with money, as he managed a dark, "Guess I'll be staying home all weekend since I'm flat broke," and trudged out the door.

She would love to be more generous and give her son spending money. There were two reasons she didn't. One, she was watching her funds closely, and having just laid out 168 dollars for the plumber, she was feeling the need to be more frugal. Second, she didn't think that giving Lucas money would be helpful to his overall situation. He'd lost his paying job because of his poor work ethic and terrible attitude. He needed to feel the consequences of those actions.

So, she didn't offer him money.

But his foul mood had dampened her own. She spilled a cup of coffee, breaking her favorite cup. After cleaning up the mess, she stared out her back windows at a sky that was dark and brooding. Rain was necessary, but did it have to come today, when she needed to see some sunshine?

"You are acting like a child, Hope Lambright," she whispered to herself. "Chin up."

John had harnessed Oreo to the buggy, and she managed to get Isaac to school despite the pressing clouds. She drove on to the market and made her way to the buggy parking area.

The crowds were smaller—no doubt owing to the impending rain. Yet a surprising number of people still attended the vendor booths, sporting bright umbrellas and raincoats. As Hope hurried toward the main building, she tried to think positive thoughts about the encroaching storm. Possibly, with the turn in the weather, Amos would work in the office with her that day. It would feel like old times.

He did work inside that day. She supposed less help was needed out on the grounds when the crowds were smaller. But he didn't work in their office. Instead, he took his work down to the conference room and spread it out there, explaining every item to Lucas, what he needed to do with it and the process for completing the paperwork. Hope knew this was what he did because she popped in to offer coffee and cookies.

Lucas looked disinterested and Amos didn't quite meet her gaze.

She felt foolish and a little embarrassed, so she returned to her office and attacked the small pile of filing left to complete with a vengeance. By the time the dark clouds outside let loose with a downpour of rain, the weather matched her mood.

It rained most of the afternoon.

Lucas left an hour before her, since his workday started

earlier than hers did. "You could wait and ride home with me," she suggested.

He looked at her as if she'd spoken to him in a foreign language.

"Ride with me. In the buggy. Instead of getting wet."

Lucas shook his head, slouched into his secondhand jacket and walked out into the rain. It hurt her to look out the window and watch him walk away. She felt like she was losing a little part of herself.

"Something's bothering him."

Hope nearly jumped out of her apron.

"Didn't mean to startle you," Amos said.

"Didn't hear you come up." They both turned to watch Lucas trudge through the downpour. "He doesn't even bother with trying to stay dry."

"Such things matter less to some teens."

She turned to study him then. Hope didn't understand why Amos had decided to take a step back from their relationship. She was tempted to ask him what she'd done wrong. But a part of her was more mature than that. Deep in her heart, Hope understood that it wasn't the right time for them.

"I thought I was making progress," Amos admitted. "Earlier in the week he seemed interested, but yesterday afternoon his mood took a sour turn, and today I don't think he heard a word I said."

"You're not...not going to fire him again. Are you? Because losing another job—"

"Nein." Amos placed a hand on her arm, then jerked it back and fiddled with his suspenders. "I committed to being his mentor. I wouldn't let a bad day or two change that commitment. Let's hope tomorrow is better."

"Ya. Let's hope it is."

She couldn't explain her middle son's attitude. She'd never understood it herself. She would have loved to have shared her worries and her questions with someone. Keeping everything bottled up inside was not a healthy way to cope with pressure.

"Is Isaac around?" Amos asked.

"*Nein*. John got off early due to the weather. He stopped by and took him home."

"That makes sense."

They stood there for a moment, watching one another without directly staring. Waiting. Finally, Amos said goodnight and walked away.

Hope felt an inexplicable urge to weep.

In that moment, she admitted to herself how much she missed their talks. More than any of the other small issues this week, that was the problem she was dealing with. That was what fouled her mood much more than a day of rain.

It wasn't the cost of the plumbing; it was that she had no one to tell about it. She'd solved the problem of carting the rabbit and hutch home—at least she hoped she had—but she wanted someone to laugh with about it. And Lucas's attitude was nothing new, but she wanted to share her fears with someone.

She hadn't told Amos about Edwin's letters. She dreaded opening her mailbox every day, afraid there would be another there, still uncertain how to handle the entire situation. She would have liked to have asked him that, but there never seemed to be an appropriate time. Her problems weren't his.

Still…

Amos had a way of listening that indicated he cared. He had the kindest eyes. What she missed more than anything, even more than the possibility of a romantic relationship, was Amos's friendship.

And that was something, even if she found a dozen other friends, that she wasn't sure she'd be able to replace.

Chapter Eleven

Amos spent Thursday going to local-area farms, where he assessed possible auction items. "This is something Gideon usually does," he explained to Lucas.

"So why are we doing it?"

"This summer's crowds will be quite large. Every week brings unprecedented growth and new challenges. Gideon needed to stay on property today, so I offered to handle this."

Lucas squirmed in his seat, something Amos was learning to interpret as him actually showing interest.

"Do you have a question?"

"Ya."

"You'll only learn the answer if you ask it."

"I thought you were the boss."

"The boss?"

"You're the general manager. Doesn't that make you the boss?" There was none of Lucas's normal attitude in the question. "What I mean is, don't you tell other people what to do?"

"Ah. I see what you're saying." He waited a moment before answering. He was also learning that with Lucas, it was best to have pauses. It wasn't that the boy was slow to understand—in fact, the opposite was true. In most cases, he caught on quickly. But too much information at once seemed to cause him to shut down.

"As the general manager, I'm responsible for what does or doesn't work at the market. I suppose that does make me the boss, but a good boss looks for ways to make his business run more efficiently."

"Is that why we did all that paperwork yesterday?"

"It is. Gideon attended to the antique auction yesterday."

"I'd like to see that—the antique auction, I mean. Not sure why people would pay extra for old stuff."

"Excellent. We'll make a point of going in there next week."

Which seemed to satisfy Lucas.

They stopped by four different farms. The first was owned by an *Englisch* couple planning to have an estate sale.

"We're moving to Florida," Jebb Taylor explained. "Our daughter has found us a nice condo there."

"Won't be the same," his wife, Bonnie, admitted. "But it will be warm and sunny all year."

The furniture on offer included good pieces Amos thought would bring in a nice amount. But the real find was the glassware. He'd seen those pieces go for more than what the furniture would fetch. The couple signed the contract, and Amos told them someone would be by the next day to pick up what they felt good about auctioning.

The second farm was Amish—though Philip Gold attended a different church congregation. He had quite a few antique farming tools lying around the area outside his barn.

"We'll take them," Amos said. "And we should be able to get you a good price."

The third farm belonged to a younger *Englisch* couple who collected vintage toys.

"I was selling them on eBay," Jocelyn Carter explained, placing a hand on her protruding stomach. "Now with the babies coming—twins—I don't think I'll have time."

Again, they made arrangements for someone to pick up the items. As they were headed back toward the main road, Lucas said, "Seems we could have taken those with us. May have saved someone a trip."

"Maybe," Amos agreed. "I've done that a few times, but more often than not, the person has a bigger stash than they've initially shown us. Sometimes they're embarrassed that they've let the sheer amount of items grow out of control. After they've thought about it a day or two, they'll often add more items to the auction. Because of that, it's easier and more time efficient to let Brady Schultz pick it up in his panel truck."

Brady was an *Englischer* who worked at the market. His truck, driving license and dependability made him a wonderful employee—something Amos shared with Lucas.

They were at the final farm for the day when Lucas's mood took a dramatic downward turn. It, too, was an *Englisch* farm. The elderly gentleman who lived there took them inside his barn and waved toward the far wall. Leaning against it were at least a hundred vintage advertising signs—everything from *Drink Coca-Cola* to Williams' Soap to Gold Medal Flour.

"I've seen these sell well before," Amos told him. "I think it would be best to take twenty at a time, and I'd like to take one back today to show my head auctioneer."

"Sounds good."

Amos looked around for Lucas as he carried a metal Wonder Bread sign to the buggy. He was surprised to find the boy sitting in the buggy already, staring down at his hands, a frown on his face. He tried to get Lucas to talk on their way back to the market, but received only one-word answers.

"Think we'll knock off early today. Want me to drop you at your house?"

Lucas shrugged.

Amos wanted to call him on it, wanted to remind him to use his words and look directly at someone, but he couldn't. Something was troubling Lucas, and he wasn't ready to talk about it. Amos dropped him off, then considered going to the market and speaking to Hope about it.

With only a little more than a month left to work at the market, he'd been intentionally spending less time in his own office. He knew that wasn't the answer. No matter how little or how much he saw Hope, he thought about her often. Still, maybe time would heal the ache in his heart. And it was an ache. He'd allowed himself to dream about another family, and now he was left with a future as bleak as the day before he'd met her. How was that possible? How could a dream blossom so quickly? And what was he going to do about it?

Lost in thought, he turned his mare toward home.

Perhaps some time working in the yard would raise his spirits.

Earlier in the week, he'd promised to attend the children's pageant at the Amish schoolhouse in town that was to be held that evening. The teacher was one of the young ladies who had worked at his market when she was a teen. She'd married a Mennonite fellow over in Goshen and had been a teacher for many years. Unlike Amish, Mennonite teachers usually stayed on even after they'd had children. Sadie Miller was in her late thirties, and her children attended the same schoolhouse where she taught.

Amos knew it also was the same school young Isaac went to. Isaac would be there, as would his mother and brothers. He'd need to fortify his determination to keep things on a *friends only* basis between himself and Hope—no reaching for her hand or asking her to ride in his buggy. But he wouldn't run away. Matters of the heart weren't something that could be outrun. You had to find a way to live with them.

So he went home, trimmed rose bushes, brushed the mare, took a book and a glass of tea to the porch. But he never opened the book. Instead, he sat there, staring out over his farm and thinking about how things couldn't satisfy the heart—only people could do that.

Isaac was beside himself with excitement. Not only did he have a poem to recite in the end-of-school program, but they were bringing Hoppy home for the first month of summer.

"I said we could keep him all summer, but Mrs. Miller reminded me that it's important to share. Lilly Fisher…you remember I told you about her…she gets Hoppy for the month of July. Still, that gives us almost five weeks. It's going to be great. Right? Can I say my poem to you again?"

Hope tried to encourage Isaac even as she made a quick dinner and worried that John and Lucas wouldn't make it home. They did—John in time to eat dinner, Lucas in time to walk with them to the little schoolhouse. Isaac pulled the red wagon, which now didn't look nearly big enough for a rabbit hutch. John had assured her they'd somehow make it work.

"In Lancaster, we had an end-of-year picnic," John said. "I wonder why they do it different here."

"Because Mrs. Miller is leaving to see her family in Texas." Lucas hopped ahead, then ran back to them. "She says we'll have the traditional picnic next year."

The schoolhouse and Mrs. Miller had been a bright spot in their move. Hope liked the teacher, and Isaac had responded well to her strict but kind demeanor. She wasn't at all surprised to see a good turnout of students, parents and families. The area around the schoolhouse was filled with buggies, bicycles and even pony carts.

It was a surprise to see Amos standing at the school-house door talking to Mrs. Miller. Isaac flew up the stairs and threw his arms around Amos. "Where have you been, Amos? I haven't seen you in forever."

A look that might have been guilt passed over Amos's face. He met Hope's gaze, smiled tightly, then bent to say something to Isaac. Mrs. Miller was encouraging everyone to find a seat so the program could begin. Hope was a bit distressed when Isaac insisted on the entire family sitting with Amos. Of course, feeling embarrassed about that was silly. She couldn't avoid the man in a town as small as Ship-she, especially when he was her boss.

Not for long though.

Her job was up July 1—there were thirty-two days left, and those days were ticking away quickly. She pushed that thought away, determined to enjoy Isaac's last day of school.

The children opened with three songs. Hope couldn't help smiling, and when she glanced over at Amos, he was beaming nearly as big as she was. Next they had readings about summer and farming, which included Isaac's reading, a poem by Robert Frost entitled "Fireflies in the Garden." For a moment, Hope forgot her problems and enjoyed listening to her youngest child recite the poem. There were small skits, more singing and the presentation of Mrs. Miller's gift—a new schoolbag stuffed full with school supplies for the following year.

More quickly than seemed possible, the program was over. Isaac dashed toward them. "Did you hear me?"

"We did," John said. "Nice job, little bro."

"Where's Lucas?" Isaac asked.

Hope only realized at that moment that he wasn't with them. Where had he gone? He'd been sitting beside her during the program. Perhaps he'd seen a friend and gone to speak to them? Amos again met her gaze and something passed between them. A shared worry?

He turned to Isaac and said, "Heard there are cookies here somewhere."

"Sure are!" Isaac was easily distracted.

"Danki," she whispered to Amos as they made their way to the refreshment table.

"Gem gschehne," he replied with a smile.

And with that smile, something in Hope's heart melted. Her hesitancy? Her worry over what was right and what was wrong? Her embarrassment? Whatever it was, it wasn't worth coddling. This man was too important to her.

John had moved on to talk to a pretty girl who looked to be his age. They acted as if they knew each other well.

"That's Miranda," Amos said in a low voice. *"Gut* girl. I think she works at JoJo's Pretzels, so no doubt John has met her."

Hope couldn't help smiling. "Thanks for keeping an eye out for my children, Amos."

They'd reached the refreshment table. Several of the older students were standing behind it, helping replenish plates when they grew empty. Apparently, one of the girls was the person who had helped with Isaac's grade, as was so often done in one-room schoolhouses.

"Mary, this is Amos." Isaac hopped from foot to foot. "I told you about him. He's sort of like my *grossdaddi*. Aren't you, Amos?"

Hope was looking at Amos when Isaac said this. At the word *grossdaddi*, a pained expression flashed across his face, though he quickly recovered. Was that what this was about? Was he offended by the word *grossdaddi*? That made no sense, since he had several *grandkinner*. Or was it something else?

Did Amos think he was too old for her?

Did he think he was too old for her children?

Amos laughed and changed the subject, but Hope didn't forget what had happened.

After he'd helped them load the hutch onto the platform on the back of his buggy—the wagon never would have worked—John and Isaac walked home. Amos and Hope rode in the buggy. They didn't make small talk, and she was grateful for that. Because it was time to tell Amos what was in her heart. It was time to be truthful. She was too old for this kind of relationship drama, especially if things could be cleared up with one embarrassing conversation.

The worst that could happen was her being wrong about how he felt. *Nein*, the worst that could happen was that he'd laugh at her. But Hope knew Amos better than that. He would never laugh at her over matters of the heart.

The boys unloaded the hutch and set it up in the backyard. By that time, Isaac was nearly sleeping on his feet.

"I'll get him to bed," John offered. "Then I'm going out for a little while."

Hope couldn't resist asking, "This wouldn't have anything to do with the nice girl you were talking to at the school, would it?"

"Never could get anything past you." He grinned, said goodbye to Amos and headed in to settle Isaac.

"I should be leaving too," Amos said.

"I'd rather you didn't."

Amos froze, almost causing Hope to laugh. *Like a rabbit in a snare*, she thought.

"Could we talk for a moment?"

"Uhh…"

"Don't look so worried, Amos. It's just two friends talking. Okay?"

"Right. Okay. Sure, we can. Of course."

"Hot tea?"

"That would be nice."

"Stay here. I'll be back in a few minutes."

Amos settled into one of the two rockers that had mysteriously appeared in her backyard. Hope thought that she could get used to Shipshewana. She could be happy here. The community was kind and generous. The school was good. She liked her job, and when it was over, she'd find another.

She made two cups of herbal tea and brought them out to the rockers. Before Amos could make an attempt at small talk, she launched into her questions.

"I want to know why you've been different with me."

"Different?"

"What changed?"

He stared into his tea.

"I think you care for me, Amos." His head jerked up. His eyes met hers. "And I care for you. So what happened? What changed since you kissed me by the lakeside?"

He smiled then. "That's a precious memory for me, Hope."

"But?"

He sipped the tea and seemed to be having trouble organizing his thoughts, so she asked gently, "Do you think you're too old for me, Amos? Too old for my boys?"

This time when he looked at her, there was a sadness in his gaze that she longed to wipe away.

"Is it that obvious?"

"It was when Isaac introduced you as *grossdaddi*."

Amos squeezed his eyes shut, then sighed. "*Ya*. That sort of drove the point home."

"But we're not going to throw something special away because of the misunderstandings of a child. Right?"

"What if I am too old for you?"

"What if you're not?"

For the next half hour, they talked candidly about their worries, their fears, their hopes.

Amos confessed he worried that he wouldn't be able to do the things that young fathers did. Hope pointed out he already was doing those things—playing catch with Isaac, working on small projects around the house, taking the time to listen to John's worries about becoming an adult, mentoring Lucas.

Finally, Amos admitted that he thought she deserved someone her own age. She explained that she didn't want someone else and she didn't care about age.

"I want you, Amos. I care for you."

"Why?"

"Why? Seriously?" She did laugh then—a small, soft, joyous thing. "Because you're kind, generous, dependable... but mostly because my heart tells me you're the person who could become a part of my life. The question is simple—do you feel the same?"

"I do."

"So let's give this a chance. I've been miserable the last few weeks."

"Same."

"Neither of us are young chickens. We don't have time to waste."

Amos laughed at that. "True enough."

When they finally stood, he pulled her into his arms, and Hope felt as if she'd finally come home. How was it that she could feel so comfortable with him? How could her heart be so certain of this? Neither had said they loved the other, but she thought—she was *sure*, as he gently kissed her, then took her hand and walked with her to his buggy—that soon they would.

All they needed was a little time and a little space to explore this relationship. The absence of drama. A chance to spend time alone together.

Alas, that was not meant to be.

Saturday they went on a family picnic together—Hope, Amos and Isaac.

Sunday was church services. That evening she pulled another page off the wall calendar. June had arrived. She had a job for thirty more days. She still hadn't answered Edwin's letters. Nothing was more certain than it had been a week earlier—nothing except her feelings for Amos and his feelings for her.

On Tuesday, Lucas quit his job. According to Amos, he said, "This isn't for me," and walked away.

He didn't go home.

He didn't explain himself.

He simply disappeared.

Chapter Twelve

When Hope went to bed on Tuesday evening, she was a little worried and a little angry. How could Lucas have thrown away another chance? What was he thinking? And what was he planning to do next?

She somehow managed to sleep, but when she woke the next morning and Lucas still wasn't home, her worry turned to dread. Had he been hurt? Had he been arrested?

John walked into the kitchen as she poured her second cup of coffee. "Still no sign of him?"

"Nope."

"I'll ask around at work. Check if anyone has seen him."

"That would be helpful."

"Mamm, whatever it is…" He ran a hand over his face and attempted—unsuccessfully—to stifle a yarn. "Whatever he's done, it's not your fault."

"Doesn't make it any easier though." She turned her gaze toward the backyard, thought of Amos enjoying dinner there with them, thought for just a moment of how life could be.

"Worry ends where faith begins."

She turned to her oldest, eyebrows raised, a smile tugging at her lips. "You're quoting Amish proverbs to me?"

"*Ya.* I guess so. That's one my *mamm* likes to say."

He gave her an awkward hug, then both went to get ready for work.

What should she do next? Go to the market? Go to the police? Stay home and wait for him? She kept deciding on one path only to question it and wonder if that was the wrong thing to do. In the end, it was a decision she didn't have to make alone. Amos pulled up just after John had left.

She met him at the door. Her chin began to quiver when he studied her with those knowing eyes, and then he pulled her into an embrace and she let the pent-up tears fall. He didn't admonish her, tell her to pull herself together or awkwardly pat her back. He held her, let her cry and seemed to understand the depth of her grief.

Once she'd stepped back and dried her eyes, he held up a pastry bag. "Thought a muffin might help."

They sat at the kitchen table as sunshine poured over the backyard.

They discussed their options.

Their options. "Lucas is your son, Hope. How you proceed from here is your decision. But, if you'll let me, I'd like to stand beside you and support you during this time. I'd like it to be something we go through together."

How long had she waited to hear those words?

By the time Isaac joined them at the table, they'd come up with a plan.

"Donut holes?" Isaac asked, a smile spreading across his face. "For me?"

Hope reached over and messed his hair. "With milk, please."

"Sounds *gut*." He hopped out of the chair, gave his mom and then Amos a quick hug, and hurried over to the refrigerator.

Thirty minutes later, they'd dropped Isaac off with Eunice, who was happy to have him stay at her house for the day. Then they started in on their list.

There was still no sign of Lucas at the market. They checked with Gideon, the parking attendant, and everyone else they saw.

"I'll get the word out," Gideon said. "Amos, I'll call you on the cell phone if anyone hears anything."

Next they drove over to the Cove, a youth recreation center, but there were no teens there so early in the morning. They were able to talk to the woman working the front desk, who knew Lucas but hadn't seen him since the night before.

"He came in with the crowd he runs with." Her eyes darted left, then right, and finally settled on Hope. "I guess you know about that."

"I had hoped the association had stopped, but apparently it hasn't."

The woman's expression softened. "Children have no idea how much they worry us until they have children of their own."

"Can you give us any names?" Amos already had a pen and paper in hand. He wrote down the three names she knew for certain—all Amish. "We should take this to Ezekiel next."

Ezekiel listened as they told him what had happened the day before and what they'd done so far to look for Lucas. "I'll take this family." He pointed to the top name on the list. "The other two live fairly close together on the opposite side of town."

"We'll take those," Amos said.

"And we'll meet back here." Ezekiel paused and put a hand on both Hope's shoulder and Amos's. "*Gotte* hasn't forgotten our Lucas. We will continue to pray for his safety and that soon he will come home."

It felt like more than a prayer.

It felt like a heartfelt cry for help, wrapped in the certainty that *Gotte* hadn't forgotten or forsaken them.

"You look a bit pale," Amos said when they were back in the buggy. "Maybe the sugary muffin and more coffee weren't the right thing. Would you like to stop for some real food?"

"I couldn't eat anything else." Her eyes met his. *"Danki."*

"Of course."

It was a long day. By the end of it, Hope felt as if she were sleepwalking through thick molasses. Just picking up her feet took great effort. No one had seen Lucas. The other boys he hung around with were all accounted for, but they didn't know for certain where Lucas was. One told them that Lucas might have left on a bus.

"Would he have gone back to Lancaster?" Amos asked when they were back at the house on Walnut Lane—just the two of them and a list that had each line scratched out.

"Nein. There's no one there."

"Maybe you should call the bishop all the same."

"Right. Yes. I will do that." She stood and found her coin purse, prepared to walk down to the phone booth.

Amos stopped her, slipped his cell phone into her hand and murmured, "I'll give you some privacy."

But Lucas hadn't been seen in Lancaster either. It was an eleven- or twelve-hour bus ride, depending on the stops. He should have been there by now if he'd left the night before.

She joined Amos on the front porch, hugging her arms around herself, trying to hold herself together. Despite the warmth from the afternoon sun, a chill ran through her. "Our bishop from Lancaster will call Ezekiel if anyone sees Lucas."

"Are you going to be okay here tonight?"

"Yes."

"Would you like one of my girls to come and stay with you?"

"That's not necessary." Her words were a whisper, but she felt as if she were about to fly apart. Amos's arms around her helped. She breathed more deeply, became aware of her feet against the porch floor, the breeze in the trees, the occasional car or buggy passing on the street.

Finally, she stepped back. "I don't know how to say how much of a help you've been. I can't even imagine how I would have handled this alone."

Amos waited until she raised her gaze to meet his. "You're a strong woman, Hope. There is no doubt in my mind you would have handled it alone with grace and faith and optimism. But you don't have to do that. You don't have to handle anything alone again if you don't want to."

Her breath caught in her throat.

Amos kissed her softly, then stepped back and donned his hat. "We'll speak of this more, after Lucas is home."

She nodded, then went into the house.

She should start dinner. Isaac would be home soon. Eunice had promised to drop him off late in the afternoon. John would return from his shift. Life didn't stop because of tragedy or loss.

You don't have to handle anything alone again if you don't want to.

There was a promise in Amos's words, in his voice, in his eyes. This had been the worst day of her life, worse even than the day they'd found Daniel.

The day they'd found Daniel...

She tried not to dwell on that, but now she forced herself to remember. It had been at the beginning of summer. Maybe even the first week the boys had been out of school. The first week of June. Two years ago, this week.

Was that why Lucas had fled? Had the anniversary of his father's death somehow sent him running? Hope wasn't sure, but it was one more thing she'd talk to Amos and Ezekiel about. For too long she'd lived in the shadow of Daniel's deeds and his death. The letters in her suitcase proved that. Why had she kept it all a secret? What hadn't she asked for help?

Somehow she'd always suspected that Daniel's life would end suddenly. Tragically. But Lucas? He'd been her happy toddler. He'd never gone through the terrible twos. It was only when he hit the teenage years that he'd faltered.

You don't have to handle anything alone again if you don't want to.

She didn't want to. She admitted to herself in that moment that she was tired of being strong. She was tired of doing things alone. She was ready to accept help and she was ready to say yes to the promise in Amos's eyes.

The next day Amos accompanied Hope as she filed a missing persons report with the Shipshewana Police Department. It would help to have the *Englischers* looking for Lucas. The officer was sympathetic and assured Hope that these situations usually resolved on their own. But the young woman was also direct. "It often takes time before a teen finds his way back home—sometimes months. Don't give up hope. And we'll have our officers keep an eye out."

June insisted on being beautiful, vibrant and full of life, despite the tragedy unfolding around Hope.

A week passed, then two.

Still, they heard nothing.

Amos's heart broke anew for Hope every day.

Ezekiel sent out word to surrounding church districts, but Elkhart and Lagrange Counties held the oldest and largest Amish communities in the state of Indiana—more than two hundred congregations that were roughly twenty-eight thousand members strong. Finding a teenage boy wouldn't be easy, especially if he didn't want to be found.

They began attending Noah's meetings together—Hope and John and Amos. One meeting was designed for younger siblings and so they brought Isaac along. Though it didn't feel like a time for celebrating, it was a fine summer day. Isaac stepped out of the meeting place and declared, "Man. Feels like a day for ice cream."

Amos couldn't hold in a snicker. John laughed. Even Hope smiled, and so they went to Howie's. Was Hope remembering their first date there? Hard to believe it had been less than two months ago. Hard to believe that he'd been foolish enough to think he could decide not to love her.

They were settled at one of the picnic tables with their ice creams when Isaac surprised them again. "He'll come home. Do you know how I know? Because he loves Oreo. Told me she was the finest horse he'd ever seen. He'll come home for Oreo, even if he's mad at us."

Which led to an open discussion about why Lucas might have left, how it wasn't anyone's fault, how they each believed he would return. It was the first day with any sense of normalcy. They went back to Hope's and worked in the vegetable garden that Hope and John had started.

Hope stood there surveying the results of their labor—tomato plants staked to a trellis, okra, squash, bell peppers, onions, radishes, snap beans and green beans, all surrounded by rows of herbs and flowers.

"Looks *gut*," she declared.

"I think so, too." Isaac cocked his head. "Can't say I'm

excited about those snap bean plants…they're fun enough to snap, but I don't much like eating them."

"We'll cook them with bacon and herbs," Hope assured him. "You'll like them this year."

"Makes my stomach growl just looking at it," John said.

"I can second that." Amos grinned at John, and something passed between them. An unspoken thank-you. An acknowledgment that they both cared for the woman who would be cooking the majority of the meals from the plants in front of them. "Actually, I'm not a bad cook myself. I didn't plant one at my place, but all of my *doschdern* planted big gardens behind their homes."

"Between us, we'll keep you in fresh vegetables." Hope smiled, then turned toward the house. "Anyone want to help me set out our dinner?"

Hope had cooked a chicken in the oven. All four of them traipsed inside and then back out to the picnic table—carrying plates and glasses, forks and knives, chicken, corn, salad and fresh bread. They enjoyed an early dinner sitting at the picnic table between the garden and the house. John and Isaac cleaned up the dishes, and then Isaac challenged Amos to a game of checkers. John left to pick up a girl.

"There's music in the park starting at eight. It might be late when I get home." He kissed his *mamm*, thanked Amos for his help, and then it was just Isaac, Amos and Hope.

Amos picked up the *Budget* and set to reading it as Hope herded Isaac into his bath, made sure he'd cleaned behind his ears and rinsed his hair and reminded him to hang his towel on the rack.

When they walked out of the bathroom, Isaac looked at his mom and then Amos. "Anyone want to read with me? Just a chapter?"

Was ten years old too old for such?

Amos didn't think so.

He was pretty happy when Isaac handed him the book.

By the time he made it back into the sitting room, Hope had set out two hot cups of tea and a platter of oatmeal raisin cookies. "Made with applesauce, so I think you can have two."

He sat beside her on the couch, savored the cookie, sipped the tea. "I've missed this," he finally said.

"This?"

"All of it." He waved his hand around the room—to the checkerboard that sat waiting for another game, to Isaac's room, to them. Placing his cup on its saucer, he sat forward, clasped his hands together and tried to think of how to put into words all that was in his heart. "I spent years worrying that my girls wouldn't marry. It wasn't that I wanted to rush them off, but I had convinced myself that they needed to begin their own lives."

"And now?"

"Now they have. I couldn't be happier about that."

When he didn't continue, she added, "But…"

He laughed, sat back and studied this woman who had become so precious to him. "I didn't count the cost. I didn't realize how lonely life would be. I didn't understand, until Eunice married and left our home, that I had also moved on to a different phase of my life."

"No one expects to enter those years alone."

"True, yet it happens sometimes." He raised his hands, then dropped them. "I won't begin to second-guess God, though I went through denial, anger, bargaining, depression—"

"And finally acceptance." Hope nodded. "Stages of grief. It's never easy, Amos. It certainly wasn't easy for me, and I gather it wasn't for you."

"Which is one reason that you've been such a special addition to my life. You understand what it's like to be alone. You understand how precious it is to have a helpmate at your side."

"I do."

Amos reached for her hand. "I realize that now isn't the best time to..."

He closed his eyes, heard Hope whisper, "Or maybe it's the perfect time."

So he opened his eyes, held both of her hands in his and finally shared what was on his heart. "I love you, Hope. I want to spend the years I have left with you. At first I thought that you deserved someone younger, but I've spent a lot of time thinking on it, praying on it and examining my feelings. I want to be a father to your boys—all of your boys. I want to help carry your burdens. Could you, do you think that you..."

"Love you? Yes. I could, and I do."

"Really?" Amos's final worries melted away. She loved him. She cared for him. They could do this.

"Yes, Amos. I love you. Are you surprised?"

"*Nein*. I had hoped." He kissed her softly. "Will you marry me, Hope? It doesn't have to be soon. We don't even have to set a day, but will you?"

He thought she would answer right away, expected she would throw herself into his arms. Instead, she stood, her expression serious and said, "Give me a minute."

Give her a minute?

That didn't sound good.

Amos thought he'd mastered the art of being patient, but the minute and a half she was out of the room seemed like an eternity.

She returned holding a small packet of letters. "Before we talk more about...our future... I need to be honest with you about my past. These letters are from a man named Edwin Bing. I received the first in the spring."

Hope sat beside him on the couch, pulled off the rubber band that held the letters together and fingered through them. "They began arriving a few months ago."

When she raised her eyes to his, Amos understood how difficult it was for her to talk about these things. So, instead of telling her that it didn't matter and that she shouldn't worry…instead of saying any of the things he longed to say, he replied, "Tell me more."

The story was one that he had heard before. *Englischers* liked to think that Amish were perfect. They weren't. Amish couples dealt with alcoholism, abuse, infidelity and more—all of the things that *Englisch* couples did. So what Hope told him didn't surprise him, but it did hurt his heart to hear what she'd been through. Her husband had tried many get-rich-quick schemes. The last, that she knew of, had involved signing people up to sell under him.

"Sell what?"

"I'm not sure. I never heard of any product. The person under you gives you a sum of money—in this case, three thousand dollars, and then they begin to sign people up under their name, forwarding part of the money they receive to you."

"Hope, that's a pyramid scheme."

"I don't know what that is."

"Basically it's what you describe. You earn money by enrolling others, but there isn't any real push to sell a product."

"Then I guess that's what it was." She slipped her *kapp* strings behind her shoulders, still staring at the letters in her hands. "Regardless, Daniel only enrolled one person— Edwin Bing. We never saw much of the money since Daniel had to pass part of it up the…um, pyramid. Now, more than two years later, Edwin wants his investment back. He's threatening to sue me."

"May I?" Amos reached for the letters.

"Of course."

He read every carefully, then stacked them back together, placed the rubber band around them and set them on the coffee table. "There's an attorney here in Shipshewana who is familiar with and sympathetic to our Plain ways. I would like you to take these to her and tell her what you've told me."

"Okay."

"I don't think you have anything to worry about. I don't think this person has any claim to what is yours."

"Oh." Hope glanced around the room, then back at him. "You're sure?"

"I'm pretty sure. The attorney will be able to confirm whether I'm right. Regardless, this is something that you and I will handle together."

She closed her eyes a moment, smiled softly and then threw herself into his arms. "Ask me again."

"Will you marry me, Hope Lambright?"

"I will."

They kissed once more, and then she snuggled in next to him.

"You're committing to several more years of homework with Isaac," she said.

"Yup."

"And eventually there will be a wedding for John, though I know it's much too soon to speak of such things."

"I love weddings."

"Then there's Lucas…"

"We'll find a way to help Lucas—together we will find a way."

They sat together for a few minutes, drawing strength and

comfort from one another, envisioning their future. Finally, he added, "My girls adore you."

"I'll be a *mammi*." She sat up straight. "Oh my goodness."

She stared down at her hands and began counting all of the *grandkinner* on her fingers, "Mary and Abram. Lydia."

"Baby Daniel."

"Peter. Grace. And Josh." She closed her eyes, a smile spreading across her face. "Isaac and Josh will be cousins."

"Together we'll make a big family," Amos said. "That doesn't bother you?"

"It does not, but I have some sewing to do if I'm going to have Christmas presents ready, not to mention birthdays."

Amos laughed. He was still surprised by the joy he felt when he was around Hope, the lightness in his soul, the extra little bit of energy in his step. He wanted this. He'd raised five girls, and now he wanted to help raise three boys. Mostly, he wanted to spend what time he had left with the woman sitting beside him. It wouldn't be a life free from trouble—the current situation with Lucas was proof of that. But it would be a life they would live and celebrate together.

Eight days later, they were contacted by the police.

Chapter Thirteen

In spite of Hope's personal heartache over her son…as well as her joy in being in a committed relationship with Amos, life continued as normal.

The weather in Shipshewana was similar to Lancaster. At least, so far it had been. The days were ideal, with temperatures in the eighties, and the nights were cool enough to sleep with the windows open. Evening was Hope's favorite time—those moments that separated an afternoon of solid work from a time of rest. She had cleaned up the dinner dishes and was outside watering the flowers that surrounded her front porch—a project she and Isaac had worked on together—when a Shipshewana Police Department vehicle pulled up to the curb.

A police vehicle.

Her son was still missing.

No word for weeks.

Those three thoughts hit her mind at once, along with a sense of dread she had never experienced before. Feeling as if her legs wouldn't support her, she sank onto the top porch step.

Was he dead?

Had the police found Lucas under some bridge?

Was her heart about to be torn in two?

The same officer they'd spoken to when Lucas had first gone missing stepped out of the car. Officer Lockhart offered a small wave and walked toward the porch. She didn't look as if she were about to share tragic news. An officer wouldn't wave so casually if she were about to crush a mother's heart. Would she? On the other hand, neither was she smiling.

"Mrs. Lambright."

"Officer. You've..." She gulped down her fear. "You've heard something."

"We have. Your son is fine. He's booked in the Goshen Police Department for minor in possession and public intoxication. He was arrested last night, but the paperwork wasn't processed until this morning."

Hope knew from Lucas's trouble in Lancaster that anyone arrested was routinely offered the chance to make a phone call. But how would he have called her? She didn't have a phone, and he probably hadn't memorized the closest phone shack's number. He could have called the market, he could have called Amos, but he hadn't.

"Can I see him?"

"Yes. If you'd like, we can give you a ride over."

"*Nein.* I need to call Amos. He'll contact a driver."

"All right. If you need anything from us..."

"I'll call."

Officer Lockhart nodded once, then turned to walk back to her vehicle. Before she was halfway down the path, she turned toward Hope and said, "I'm glad your son showed up, even if it is in a less-than-ideal situation."

"So am I."

The woman smiled at her once more, then left.

In the past, Hope would have jumped up and scurried about. She would have been all a flurry with motion and anxiety and fear. Not this time though. This time, she sat there, thanked *Gotte* that her son was alive and well and only a few miles away. She waited until her heart rate returned to normal, waited for her hands to stop shaking, waited until her vision had cleared from unshed tears. When she felt steady, she stood, went inside and called Isaac, who was in the backyard caring for Hoppy.

The clock on the wall showed the time to be a few minutes shy of seven. She wrote a number on a slip of paper and handed him a quarter—the customary amount donated to the payment jar in the phone booth. "Go call Amos. Tell him that I need to see him."

"That's it?"

"Yes, that's it."

Isaac shifted from foot to foot and tugged on his right earlobe. "Is this good news or bad?"

"I'm going to believe it's good."

Now he cocked his head. "It's about Lucas?"

"Yes. It is."

Isaac hugged her tightly. "I knew he'd come back," he mumbled, then dashed out the front door.

Hope went into the boys' room and pulled a clean set of clothes out of Lucas's drawer. She didn't know if they'd let him have them, but she wanted to take them just in case. Was he still wearing what he'd had on the night he'd left? Would he be hungry? They fed you in jail, but it wasn't like her home-cooked fare. She went into the kitchen, made two sandwiches from homemade bread, peanut butter and jelly. She added four oatmeal cookies and put it all into a paper bag. Then she put the paper bag and the clothes into a shoulder bag she'd fashioned from an old pair of blue jeans.

She wrote a note for John, who would be working until dark that evening.

Isaac came back and flopped onto the couch. "Amos is on his way. I ran all the way there and back."

"Danki," she said, calm and ready to meet whatever was waiting for her in Goshen.

Isaac sat up straight and smiled at her. "Lucas is coming home!"

"It may not be that simple."

"What do you mean?"

The right thing for Hope to do was be honest with her youngest son, but he was only ten years old. Sitting beside him on the couch, she said, "Lucas is in jail, in Goshen, which is a few miles from here."

"Oh." Isaac pulled on his right ear. "That's not good."

"It's not, but at least we know where he is. We can see him. And we can make a plan for him to come home."

"Okay."

"Did you finish taking care of the rabbit?"

"Nope." He popped up with the energy of a young boy. Pausing, he shifted from foot to foot.

"You can ask whatever you're wondering about."

"Am I going with you? To the jail?" He sounded both disbelieving and more than a little curious.

"Not sure. Let's see what Amos says."

"Gut idea. I'll go finish cleaning out Hoppy's hutch." He dashed out of the house.

Forty-five minutes later, Amos pulled his buggy to a stop in front of her house. She was there before he could set the brake and hop out.

"He's here?" His eyes darted left and right, as if Lucas might be hiding at the side of the house.

"Lucas is in Goshen. In jail. Officer Lockhart said that we could see him. He's been there since last night."

"Okay." Amos pulled out his cell phone, tapped a few buttons, spoke into it, then stuck it back into his pocket. "Driver will be here in fifteen minutes. I'll go release Peanut into the pasture with Oreo."

"I'm not sure what to do with Isaac."

"What do you want to do?"

"I'd rather he stay here," she admitted. "Until I can see for myself what kind of shape Lucas is in…"

"Right. And John?"

"Working late."

"How about we take Isaac to the horse and buggy tour kiosk? John's boss won't mind."

"*Gut* idea."

The entire conversation had taken place as they'd stood next to Amos's buggy. Hope didn't know what else to say, but she could use a hug so she stepped into his arms.

Amos kissed the top of her head and whispered, "We'll figure this out."

And that was when her tears spilled down her cheeks. Why? Why was she so vulnerable when she was around him? Or maybe it was that she didn't have to be strong anymore. She could lean on him, even if it was only for a moment.

Amos gave her the time she needed to compose herself, then he pastured the horse with Isaac's help while she went inside, picked up her bag of supplies as well as her purse, then locked the door as she walked outside again.

The driver arrived in a new-model double-cab truck. It was rather like climbing into a buggy. Her mind was noting the truck, the driver, the new car smell even as her heart knew that none of those things mattered at all.

Amos explained they had one local stop before going to Goshen and directed him toward downtown Shipshewana.

John was pulling up with a group of tourists when they arrived at the kiosk. One by one, they pressed cash into his hand and thanked him. He hurried over to Hope, listened carefully as she explained the situation and was nodding before she finished. "Want to ride around with me, bro?"

"Sure," Isaac said. "But I want to see Lucas too."

"You will," Hope assured him. "There's a possibility that he will come home with us, and if not, I'll take you to see him tomorrow."

That satisfied Isaac, who slipped his small hand in John's bigger one.

Hope and Amos hurried back to the driver's truck. As the driver headed out of Shipshewana, they discussed possible scenarios.

"He may be released into your custody," Amos said. "If the judge has set bail."

"How much would that be?"

"Depends on the judge, and before you say you can't afford it, I'm happy to pay whatever it takes so that Lucas doesn't have to spend another night in jail."

She didn't answer. She stared out the window, wondering if she could do this difficult thing, knowing in her heart that she had to. She had to make the hard decisions so that this could be over.

"I don't think so." She angled in the seat so she could look at Amos. "I want him home. I want that more than I can say. But what is actually best for Lucas? He needs to understand consequences, Amos. He needs to grow up."

He squeezed her hand. "It's your decision, of course. Let's hear what the officer has to say."

Goshen was a small town by *Englisch* standards, but in the darkness and the stress of the moment it looked huge to Hope. It reminded her of Lancaster. "Bigger than Shipshewana," she whispered to no one.

"Quite a bit bigger," Amos agreed. "Thirty-five thousand folks to Shipshewana's six hundred."

A good place for a teenage runaway to hide.

The driver stopped in front of the police station and said he'd be happy to give them a ride back.

"Not sure how long we'll be here," Amos admitted.

"Here's my number." The man passed over a business card. "If it's in the next hour, I'll probably still be in the area."

The police station was large and brought back memories of when Lucas had been arrested in Lancaster. That time had been a first offense. It had also been for underage drinking. The judge had let him off with a stern warning, which hadn't affected Lucas at all. That was when Hope had decided something drastic needed to be done. That was when she'd started closely reading the *Budget* for a place to move—anywhere far from the sad memories and unhealthy influences.

She'd shared all of this with Amos the week before.

He'd told her they'd had similar situations with youth in Shipshewana, and then there'd been Noah's situation. His son-in-law had spent several years in prison before he'd accepted that he needed to make major changes in his life. Had that happened the first year in prison or the last? Would Lucas require that much time? Would he take even longer to see the light?

She gave her identification card to the person working the front desk and explained that her son was being held in the jail. "May I see him?"

Officer Rodriguez looked to be middle-aged, had dark hair and a large build, but Hope focused on his kind eyes.

"Yes, ma'am," Rodriguez said. "You can see him. Let me make a copy of your identification card. Sign this ledger and then we'll take Lucas to our visiting room. It'll take a few minutes."

"Has his bail been set?" Amos asked.

The officer looked from Hope to Amos. He would assume they were married, but then again, Amos hadn't offered his identification. Officer Rodriguez focused on Hope again, his eyes raised in an unasked question. When she nodded that it was okay to share the information, he said, "Lucas hasn't seen the judge yet. That will happen tomorrow morning in the courtroom attached to this building. Judge Myra Lutz will preside. At that time, Lucas may be granted bail or he may be retained. I've seen it go both ways."

They waited in blue upholstered chairs. For a jail, the place had a nice lobby—simple furnishings, a few pastoral prints framed on the walls, clean ceramic tile flooring, magazines on one table and a corner with children's toys.

Children's toys.

How often were children brought to a jail?

She was glad they hadn't brought Isaac. Tomorrow would be soon enough for this to become a memory of his childhood. The furnishings didn't put Hope at ease. She perched on the edge of her chair. Her heart felt like a dishrag being twisted, and she hadn't even seen Lucas yet.

Ten minutes later, Officer Rodriguez ushered her back.

She left her shoulder bag with Amos.

The officer walked her down a hall then paused outside a door with a sign that said Inmate Visiting Room. "He's in a jumpsuit because his clothes were a real mess—vomit, alcohol, looked as if they hadn't been washed in some time."

"He ran away more than three weeks ago." Hope heard her own voice as if it were coming from a great distance.

"There's no doubt he's been on the street most of that time."

He opened the door, and Lucas's head jerked up.

For the briefest sliver of time, she saw a younger Lucas

in his eyes, one who hadn't yet struggled with his father's death, one who hadn't sought solace in the wrong places. Then the mask of indifference she'd grown accustomed to fell into place, and he stared down at the table.

She wanted to throw her arms around him, but everything about his body language shouted *stay away*. So, instead of pulling her son into her arms, she sat across from him. She kept her voice low and even. She didn't ask any questions, and Lucas didn't offer any answers.

Hope focused on explaining what Amos had said and what Officer Rodriguez had told them. She spelled out what his options might be. It was one of the most difficult conversations she'd ever had, and it was mostly one-sided.

Finally, she did ask questions. As his mother, as the person who would be paying his court fees, she had a right to know what had happened. But Lucas refused to answer her questions as to where he'd been, why he'd gone, what he'd planned to do. She didn't feel she had his full attention until she stood to leave.

"Where are you going?"

"Home."

"What about me?"

"You're supposed to appear before the judge tomorrow."

"I have to stay here another night?" His voice was indignant, his expression disbelieving.

Hope needed every ounce of patience at that moment. She wanted to shout at her son, to remind him that he was here because of his own actions. She wanted to ask him when enough would be enough. She didn't say or do any of those things.

Instead, she sat back down on her side of the table and reached for his hands. Lucas tried to pull away, but she held on tight until he raised his eyes to hers. "I love you, Lucas.

Your *bruders* love you. Amos cares for you. Ezekiel has been worried sick. You have a lot of people on your side."

Lucas blinked rapidly, but he didn't respond.

"You're wearing a jumpsuit with Goshen Police Department stamped on the back. You will spend the night here and face Judge Myra Lutz tomorrow. Maybe she will give you another chance. Maybe she won't—"

"What does that mean?"

"Have you not heard a word I said? It means she could send you to juvenile detention."

"She wouldn't—"

"She might."

And then she saw it—the fear in his expression that said he realized he may have stepped too far off the path. Her heart tore anew, but she held firm to her resolve to be candid with him.

"I want you to come home, Lucas, but I will admit that I'm not sure what to do next. I don't know how to—"

"Fix me?" Defiance flared in his eyes.

"How to help you, Lucas. I don't know how to help you."

She closed her eyes, breathed a silent prayer, then stood and walked out of the room.

She walked away from her son, which was possibly the hardest thing she'd ever done in her life.

Amos had thought he couldn't feel anything more deeply for Hope, but when she reappeared in the doorway to the waiting area, his heart lurched into his throat. She looked both strong and fragile, relieved and torn apart.

He led her to a chair.

"We should—" Hope waved at the door as tears cascaded down her cheeks.

Amos handed her his handkerchief. "There's no hurry to go. Take a moment."

She pulled her emotions under control and told Amos how Lucas looked—thinner, exhausted, scared.

She told him of his still-defiant attitude, of his surprise that he was being left to spend a night in jail, of his incredulity at hearing he might be sent to the local juvenile detention center.

"Hopefully that won't happen, but if it does...then we'll deal with it." Amos nodded at the shoulder bag she'd left with him. "Want to see if the officer will let you give that to him?"

"*Ya*. I do." She pulled in a deep breath, straightened her posture and approached the officer.

Amos joined her back at the counter, heard the officer tell Hope that he would see that Isaac got the clothes and the food.

"We give them three solid meals a day, but I'm sure anything extra will be appreciated." Officer Rodriguez pushed a sheet of paper across the counter. "This is information about tomorrow. Some folks find it helpful."

"*Danki.*"

"You're welcome, Mrs. Lambright."

Hope and Amos walked back outside. Although it felt like days had passed since she'd been standing on her front porch watering flowers, in fact, it was not yet nine in the evening. Amos called the driver who'd brought them from Shipshewana. He assured the man they could wait forty-five minutes. Once he'd closed the phone and slipped it into his pocket, he nodded to a café across the street.

"Coffee?"

"Maybe some decaf."

They shared a piece of fresh strawberry pie. Hope surprised him by eating her half and asking for a second cup of decaf.

"You're handling this well."

"Maybe."

"Meaning?"

"Meaning that not knowing was worse. Also, I think I've seen the light regarding my son. This situation may not have changed him—"

"Maybe it has."

"You're right. We can't really know, but it's changed me. I've come to a few conclusions."

"Such as?"

"Babying my son won't help him."

Amos nodded and waited.

"I love him, and I will do what I can for him, but I will not make excuses for his behavior."

"Sounds like tough love."

"I guess." She leaned forward, lowered her voice. "At heart, I'm a practical woman. I've had to be."

"Your boys are fortunate to have you as their *mamm*."

"Right now, my mind and heart are focusing on what will help Lucas. What will bring him to a place of peace and health and—eventually—independence. If the judge decides that's juvenile detention, then I'm okay with that."

Amos sat back now, still studying her.

"You're surprised?"

"A little."

"Because?"

"I don't know." He turned his coffee mug left, then right. "A part of me expected you to be emotional, to want to swoop in and cover him with your mama wings."

Instead of arguing, Hope smiled. It was a smile tinged with sadness, but it was a smile nonetheless. "A small part of me still wants to do that. But these last few weeks, going to Noah's meetings, listening to the other parents there, and speaking with Noah's parents…all those things have helped me see that I have to put what my son needs before what my heart wants to give him."

Amos cleared his throat, then tapped the sheet of paper they'd been reading—the one Officer Rodriguez had given them. "This says that it would be best to have Lucas's support group at the hearing."

"What are you thinking?"

"That we should bring Isaac and John. Also Ezekiel. Myself. And maybe even Noah."

"I think that's a *wunderbaar* idea."

"This Judge Lutz needs to understand that there is a solid family standing behind Lucas. If she still rules to place him in juvenile detention, then fine—we'll set up a visitation schedule. But if she sees us, sees the support he has and decides to give him a chance at home, then we will be that. We will be his support system—and yours."

"*Gut* plan."

Amos's phone buzzed at that moment. He had to admit the cellular contraptions came in handy during emergencies, but he'd be happy when his quit ringing. After tapping in a text, he said, "Driver's here."

He called Ezekiel as they were headed back to Shipshewana, then reached for Hope's hand and covered it with his own. "Ezekiel will meet us at your place in the morning."

"And Noah?"

"I'll stop by his place on my way home."

By the time they were dropped off in front of Hope's place, she was dead on her feet. She rallied when the front door was thrown open and John and Isaac tumbled out. Together,

Amos and Hope went inside and explained what was happening, as well as what they were going to do the next day.

John was nodding before he'd even finished talking. "My boss said to take the day off if I needed to. He said family comes first."

"I'll wear my Sunday clothes," Isaac offered.

"We all will."

Amos was relieved to see everyone agreed on the plan. Twenty minutes later, he was in his buggy, headed toward Noah's. It was nearly eleven by the time he pulled down his own lane, released Peanut into the pasture, updated Becca and Gideon, and fell into his bed.

When was the last time he'd been up so late?

It didn't bother him as much as it might have. Yes, he was tired, but he was also glad that finally this situation was moving forward. Hope had said that not knowing was worse. Amos thought that was true. Together, they could do what needed to be done. The question was whether Lucas was willing to change.

Instead of going to sleep, he lay in his bed and prayed for Lucas, prayed for Hope and John and Isaac, prayed for Ezekiel and himself and Noah. They didn't know the future, but God did. Which didn't mean life was always easy, but he believed in the center of his heart that their God was good.

Amen and amen.

Chapter Fourteen

It was a sleepless night for Hope. She wasn't particularly surprised about that. How could she sleep when her son was being held in a jail cell? She lay in bed several hours, determined to give her body rest even if her mind kept circling round and round, imagining what might happen the next day.

Finally, she pulled on her robe and tiptoed to the kitchen, though her boys slept so heavily that a horse clomping through the house wouldn't have caused a stir.

It was only three in the morning, but she made herbal tea, sat at the table and poured her heart onto the pages of her journal—something she'd begun the previous week when one of the other moms at Noah's meeting had said it helped. It did, especially when she had trouble sleeping. Once she'd spilled her worries and fears and gratitude onto the page, she glanced around at her crafting supplies set up beneath the windowsills. She was too jittery to sew, but she thought knitting might calm her nerves. She'd begun working on a pale yellow-and-green blanket for the next Yoder baby. No one was pregnant at the moment, but with five *doschdern*, someone would be soon enough.

The pattern was simple, and the repetition of slipping the yarn across her needles did what tossing hadn't been able to do. Soon her eyes were drifting shut. Instead of going to bed, she lay down on the couch, which was where John found her as dawn broke across the morning sky.

"I made coffee," he said.

She thanked him, sat up and blinked several times before she thought to wonder what time it was.

"It's only seven," John assured her, pushing the steaming cup of coffee into her hands. "You're not running late."

Since Lucas's time before the judge was set for eleven, Amos had said they'd all meet at the Lambright place at ten.

"Is there anything else I should know?" John asked.

He looked so serious and wore such an expression of grave concern that it pricked Hope's heart. She was fortunate to have such a solid, supportive son. "I'm pretty sure we covered everything last night."

"When you saw Lucas, how did he seem to you?"

She sighed. "Defiant. I'm hoping another night in jail may have softened his hard shell."

"I wouldn't count on it."

"Right."

"I've tried talking to him, *mamm*. He always clams up. May as well put his hands over his ears for as much as he listens to what I have to say."

"I appreciate that you tried. We all have."

"It's not as if I claim to have all the answers, but he won't even talk about what's bothering him." John shook his head, then sipped his coffee. "Do you think it's because he found Dat?"

"I don't know. Maybe."

"It's understandable a thing like that would mess with your head. And don't get me wrong. I miss Dat, but I also think we have a chance for a *gut* life here. Why can't Lucas see that?"

"Maybe he feels he's betraying his father by moving on. If I'd met Amos a year ago, I may have felt the same."

John smiled over the rim of his cup.

"Something you want to say, son?"

"Only that I think you two make a cute couple."

She nearly spewed her coffee, which was when Isaac walked in.

"What's everybody laughing about?"

"Your older *bruder* was making fun of me and Amos dating."

"Was not. I said you're—"

"Cute. *Ya.* I got it."

"I like Amos," Isaac declared. Then added with a yawn, "Is there cereal?"

"There is, and since I need to go and get ready, I'll forego the lecture that you should be eating oatmeal."

"Awesome!" Isaac hopped off the couch and darted into the kitchen.

Hope and John shared a look of understanding.

Isaac would grow up with a *dat*. Hope and Amos hadn't set a date, but they both wanted to be married before the end of the year. They'd refused to be any more specific than that, not wanting to hurry things while Lucas was still missing.

But this…

The ball was literally in Lucas's court. Hope had played a bit of tennis when she was a teen. She understood that there was little you could do while the ball was on the opposite side of the net. You could position yourself, prepare yourself, be ready—but you had to wait until the person you were playing against sent the ball sailing back over the net. Only then could you take action.

She was prepared.

Positioned as well as she could be.

And hopefully, this morning the ball would come back into her court.

The three of them were waiting on the porch when Amos and Noah arrived together, then Ezekiel drove up. John walked over and helped them unhitch the buggies and release the horses into the small field next door. By the time they were done, a large SUV had pulled up to the curb.

Amos did the introductions. "Hope, this is Old Tom. He's been driving Amish in this area for some time."

"As well as some of the market's tours."

Old Tom didn't look all that old to Hope. He had hair on the top of his head and a clean-shaven face. The smile he sent her way immediately set her at ease.

"There's enough room for all of us?"

"Indeed there is, plus one more if your son should be returning with us."

So Amos had told him their situation. That was good. The less explaining Hope had to do the better.

Noah, John and Isaac took the back seat. Ezekiel sat up front with Old Tom. Hope and Amos took the middle-row bench seat, which left room for one more beside her.

She closed her eyes against that hope, then embraced it. There was at least a 50 percent chance that her son would be coming home today.

They spoke of normal things on the twenty-minute drive to the Goshen police station—crops, weather, tourists, who was expecting a child and who would be marrying. When Old Tom pulled into the parking area, they all trundled out. Ezekiel held up his hand. "My watch tells me we're here with plenty of time. I'd like to take a moment to pray."

They stood in a circle on the bright summer morning, outside the police station and courtroom where Hope's son waited to learn his sentence. Old Tom joined them. When they'd bowed their heads, Ezekiel's voice was strong, calm, loving. "You know our hearts this day, Lord. You know how we long to have Lucas back in our midst. And You know what will be best for him. We pray Your blessing upon this family, these friends, the officers in this building and the judge. We pray Your blessings on young Lucas and trust that You care for him even more than we do. May Your will be done on this day, and may we be strong in our faith, our service to You and our devotion for one another."

Hope wasn't the only one swiping at her eyes when Ezekiel said a soft amen. Old Tom promised to be there when they came out. John smiled and led the way. Isaac slipped his hand into hers. Amos placed his hand lightly in the crook of her other arm. Ezekiel and Noah brought up the tail of the group.

And then they were in the courtroom, and Lucas was looking forlornly at them from his place on the bench at the other side of the rather large space. Isaac lurched toward his brother, and Hope pulled him back with a soft "Not yet, son." Lucas met her gaze, then turned his attention to the front of the courtroom.

Hope had only been in a courtroom once before, when they'd had the trouble in Lancaster. Like that room, this one had dark paneling, an American flag and a state flag, and a large desk set on a two-foot riser. Next to the judge's bench was a witness box.

Hope wasn't sure what she had imagined the judge would be like. What had her nightmares conjured? Certainly nothing like the woman who took her seat behind the bench.

Myra Lutz looked to be of a similar age as Hope, maybe a little older. Her hair was a combination of blond, brunette and random strands of gray. Her gaze was serious but not cruel. She wore a stylish pair of red glasses and, of course, the black robe of a judge.

When the bailiff called, "Lucas Lambright," Hope's breath caught in her chest. Amos squeezed her hand. Isaac scooched forward to the front of his seat.

Lucas stood and moved before the judge.

"Lucas Lambright, you are fifteen years of age and reside in Shipshewana. Is that correct?"

Lucas nodded.

"I need you to respond verbally."

"Ya."

When the judge sent him a piercing look, he amended his answer to, "I do. Yes."

"I would like to summarize for you the arrest warrant provided by the Goshen Police Department. According to the arresting officer, Officer Rodriguez, he came across you sleeping on a bench under the bridge by the state highway. You tried to evade arrest, at which point the officer pursued and handcuffed you. The officer also wrote that you were belligerent, exhibited slurred speech and failed your field sobriety test. Do you agree with this summary of what happened?"

"I do."

"Under Indiana Code section 7.1-5-7-7, it is illegal for a minor to possess or consume any alcoholic beverage. This Class C misdemeanor can carry a penalty of up to sixty days in jail and a fine of up to five hundred dollars."

Six months? Hope barely heard the words *five hundred dollars*. How would she stand her son being sent away for six months?

"Since you are under eighteen years of age, this court has two options. I can officially process your case with your designation being that of a delinquent child or I can designate you as an adult. You are being charged with minor in possession, public intoxication and fleeing arrest. Lucas, do you understand the charges against you?"

"I do."

"Can you explain to this court what happened prior to when Officer Rodriguez found you?"

Hope was looking at her son's back, but she knew him so well…knew every nuance and gesture…knew whether he was feeling defiant or subdued by his posture. Now she watched him duck his head, and she dared to hope that maybe he was coming to his senses.

"I left home. A few weeks ago. Guess I got in with the wrong crowd, and next thing I knew, I was in Goshen. Didn't really know anyone. We're from Lancaster. That's where I was born." He stopped, then continued. "Lancaster is where my *dat* died, two years ago. Anyway, I didn't know my way around Goshen. Didn't know what to do. Wandered around a bit. Ate, you know, what I could find. A few people gave me money, but I used it to buy more booze. That's about it."

Judge Lutz sat back, took off her glasses and studied him. Lucas surprised Hope. Instead of slumping or staring at the floor, he stood straight and met her gaze.

Judge Lutz donned her glasses again and shuffled a few sheets of paper. "How do you plead, Lucas?"

"How do I plead?"

"Innocent or guilty?"

"*Ya*. I'm guilty of those things."

"All right." Judge Lutz looked out over the scattering of people in her courtroom. "Who is here in support of Mr. Lambright?"

They stood as one—Hope and Amos, John and Isaac, Ezekiel and Noah.

"Come forward, please, and tell me how you're related to this young man."

Hope explained that she was his mother and that John and Isaac were his brothers. Ezekiel said he was the bishop of everyone in the group. Amos explained to the judge that he was a close friend of the family and Lucas's employer. Noah said he was also Lucas's friend, and that he ran a group for troubled youth and their families in Shipshewana.

"I've heard of you, Mr. Beiler. You're doing good work in Shipshewana, and this court would like to thank you for that." Judge Lutz turned her attention to Amos. "Should I decide that it's in Lucas's best interest to return home, would you still be his employer, Mr. Yoder?"

"I would. Lucas is a fine employee, just one dealing with some difficult issues."

"I agree with that assessment, and it's good to know that Lucas would have employment. Since you're fifteen, Lucas, I assume you're finished with school?"

"Yes."

"Do you have any interest in pursuing the rest of your education in the *Englisch* school in Shipshewana?"

"*Nein*. I'd rather work."

"Mom, how do you feel about Lucas returning home?"

"It's what I want, what we all want." Hope's left arm had begun to shake. She pinned it to her side with her right hand, hoping the judge wouldn't notice. "But we also want Lucas to get well, and I'm not sure how to help him do that."

"I'm happy to hear you say that. This court seeks to rehabilitate rather than punish where that seems feasible. I am going to release Lucas to your care, Mrs. Lambright. He will perform one hundred and fifty hours of community service, and he will be required to attend weekly counseling sessions. Lucas, I would rather not see you in my court again."

He nodded, his gaze swiveling between his family and

the judge. She hit her gavel and said, "Dismissed. Next defendant, please."

Hope closed her eyes. She heard John and Isaac rush over to Lucas. She was aware that the next defendant was being led forward and Lucas was going out a side door to be processed for release. But it wasn't until Amos said, "Let's go home," that she dared to believe it was true.

Her son was coming home.

When Amos's girls were young, they all went through a stage of going to the local library and returning with romance novels. Quick to point out the Christian fiction label on the side, they'd insisted that it was a harmless way to pass time. And the stories had seemed to make his girls happy. He'd find Ada huddled with Bethany, laughing about a plot point or turn of events in a novel. One time he'd asked them what was so funny, and they'd explained with enthusiasm how all of the heroine's problems had been solved in the last few pages of the novel.

HEA, Ada had declared. *Means Happily Ever After. It's what we all want.*

Indeed.

But this wasn't that.

Hope's troubles did not resolve the day Lucas came home. The boy began attending therapy sessions with a counselor in Middlebury. He also attended Noah's meetings at his mother's insistence. Most days he sat through those meetings quietly and did not contribute. Instead he stared out the window. He spent ten hours a week on his community service hours—sometimes picking up trash, other times helping at the animal shelter, where Ada always bragged about how good he was with the animals. Since his *mamm* insisted that he spend forty hours a week constructively, that left thirty hours for him to work with Amos.

Amos admitted that the market was not the ideal place for Lucas. They tried to involve him in the decision to work somewhere else, but Lucas had started on a new medicine to help with his depression and he had little to contribute. Mostly he wanted to sleep. His therapist and his doctor both advised they give the medicine time. "It often takes thirty to sixty days before we see a difference," the doctor had cautioned Hope.

It was a warm day in July, when Amos was sitting in Hope's backyard, watching Isaac and his friends play an informal game of baseball, that he shared his plan.

"You'll retire from the market?" Hope's eyebrows had shot up and she was leaning forward.

"Don't look so surprised. I'd planned for my retirement date to be July 1, and that day has already come and gone."

"I remember." She smiled and squeezed his hand. "I was worried my job would only last a little while."

"You're a natural. Gideon would be a fool to let you go, and Gideon's no fool—trust me."

"Why would you retire now?"

"I think that the market is not the best place for Lucas. I think, maybe, he would prefer to be outside."

"Has he said that?"

"Nope."

"What makes you think so?"

She didn't doubt him. It was more that she was curious. He knew her that well now. They were that comfortable with one another. It still came as a surprise and a joy to him.

"Maybe something in his expression when he stares out the buggy window." He cleared his throat, then Amos asked what he'd been wondering about. "Was his *dat* a farmer?"

"Not much of one. He'd begin with good enough intentions, but then he'd become distracted by another plan to get rich, a plan he'd claim would bring in more money than growing and harvesting a crop." Hope shook her head, then shrugged. "It's possible that Lucas saw the other families working the land and wished that his own *dat* was doing the same."

"Maybe. I think it would be good to give this a try."

Amos didn't stay and eat dinner every evening. He wanted to give Hope and her sons time to be together without his presence. But after two or three nights away, he would invariably find himself at her door, or she'd suggest an outing to his place or the local park. The evening he shared his plans to retire, they'd gathered for dinner at the picnic table behind Hope's home—a simple meal of turkey sandwiches, fruit salad and lemon blueberry oatmeal cookies.

Once everyone had finished eating, they broached the subject of Lucas learning to farm with all three boys.

John thought it was a good idea.

Isaac asked if he could come along.

Lucas just shrugged.

"I'm afraid that won't do, son." Hope had been patient but firm with her son. He at first seemed surprised by her saying that, but he acquiesced.

They all gave him time to respond. Lucas finally said, "I guess. Maybe. I've never farmed before."

"We'll learn together," Amos said.

"You're going to teach me? Aren't you a little...old?"

Amos heard Hope's sharp intake of breath, but he patted her hand and said, "He's not wrong," in a mock whisper, which caused Isaac to laugh and John to smile. "I farmed some in my younger years. Then, as my role at the market increased, I began hiring it out. So, I'll admit it's been some time since I hitched horses to a plow. But many things have stayed the same. You know how it is with Amish, we're slow to change."

Lucas met his gaze then and offered the barest of smiles.

Amos was happy to get any response at all. He said, "Ethan…"

"Noah's *bruder*?" Isaac asked.

"Yup. And Ada's husband. Ethan is a born farmer. He's been expanding his own crops over the last few years. I think we should start by talking to him."

"Okay."

And so it was decided. He couldn't say that Lucas made a complete turnaround then either, but he took more interest in what he was doing, asked questions and seemed to lose some of the belligerent attitude.

He knew Hope's worries were further relieved when she received a report from the attorney, Adelynn Flores, about Edwin Bing. According to her, Bing had no legal standing to demand the return of his initial investment. In fact, he'd spent eighteen months of the time between investing and when the letters had begun in prison for various crimes.

"The attorney has sent a cease and desist order to his address," Hope explained. "She doesn't think we'll hear from him again."

"*Gut* news, indeed."

Things were slowly, surely falling into place. If only they could see such progress with Lucas. July turned to August, and Amos reminded himself that things took as long as they took. It was nearly September before any real change occurred in Hope's second-born son.

"I don't know what was said," Hope admitted. "But his counselor asked that we both attend with Lucas next week."

That surprised Amos. He'd never expected to be included.

If it would help Lucas, though... "Of course. Whatever the counselor thinks is best. I'm happy to tag along."

Fall was around the corner. Amos wasn't feeling pressure exactly—it was more a longing to have his family under one roof. He became more convinced every day that it was time to marry and put the little house on Walnut Street up for sale.

The next week, he went with Hope and Lucas to the counseling session.

Micah Jones, Lucas's counselor, worked in conjunction with the local Mennonite health center. Not more than thirty-five years old, he was probably the right age to get through to Lucas. Not as young as a brother. Barely old enough to be his dad. Tall, thin, with brown curly hair that touched his collar, he had an office that put everyone at ease—comfortable chairs, soft carpet, not too much clutter but not too sparsely decorated. Plants adorned the windowsill and the bank of windows looked out over an inviting courtyard.

"It's good to meet you, Amos. Hope, nice to see you again."

"We're happy to be here," Hope said.

Amos nodded. He wasn't quite sure what was expected of him, or what he should or shouldn't say, so he waited.

"First, I'd like to let you both know that I've been pleased with Lucas's progress. He's learning to verbalize some of his worries and even to admit to things that make him anxious." The counselor had been addressing all three of them, but now he turned his attention to Amos.

"The switch to farming has had a profound effect on Lucas's anxiety." Micah stopped and smiled. "Why am I speaking for you, Lucas? Tell your *mamm* and Amos how you feel about your job change."

"I like it." His gaze drifted around the room, then settled

on Amos. "Seems a better fit than the market. No offense, Amos."

"None taken."

Lucas licked his lips, drummed his fingers against the arm of the chair and went on. "Being at the market, being around so many people makes me a little jittery. I thought it was just that I was so mad about everything, but even after those feelings faded I still felt kinda…itchy."

Micah nodded in understanding, though Amos had no idea what *itchy* meant.

As if reading his thoughts, Micah explained, "Anxiety presents in different ways. Sounds can feel too loud, lights too bright and skin irritated. It's one of the many ways our minds tells our bodies to get away from a situation. For whatever reason, Lucas is more comfortable working outdoors in the fields."

Hope's brow furrowed. "Were you using alcohol to blunt those feelings?"

Lucas shrugged, but after a look from his counselor he held up a hand in the stop position. "Use my words. I know. *Ya*, maybe, Mamm. I'm not sure, but I would get all jumpy inside and I didn't know what to do with that. Sometimes a beer or three would make everything softer. Does that make sense?"

"It does. I use my knitting sometimes to slow myself down. I know blankets are cheaper to buy at the store, but my hands need time to calm my spirit."

"I walk the fields," Amos admitted. "I suppose I've done that since I was your age."

They smiled at one another, surprised to find this commonality.

Micah clasped his hands together on his desk. "Which brings us to last week's session. Lucas and I have talked at length about his time in Lancaster, about his finding his deceased father in the barn, about the grief that accompanied his father's death. But last week we had a bit of a breakthrough." Micah nodded to Lucas, indicating he should take up the story.

Lucas rubbed his palms against his pant leg, but he looked directly at Hope. He was getting better at making eye contact, which Amos took as a good sign.

"I worried it was my fault."

"Your fault?" Hope shook her head. "I don't understand."

"I was supposed to clean out the horse stall that day, and I didn't. Instead, I played ball with the neighbor kids. Dat must have come home and found it undone, and then…" Lucas pulled in his bottom lip, blinked rapidly and continued. "And then he did my job, and he died."

Hope looked from Amos to Micah to her son. Finally, she managed, "What do you think your *dat* died of, Lucas?"

"I don't know. Heart stuff. I guess. A heart attack."

"*Nein*. He didn't. Your father had a brain aneurysm."

"I don't know what that means."

"It means that he had a weak spot in the wall of a blood vessel." Hope scooched forward on her chair. "The vessel ruptured and he died within minutes. It wasn't because he was angry or because he was cleaning out a horse stall."

Lucas didn't seem to know how to answer that. He turned to Micah. "Is that true? What she said?"

"I'm not a medical physician, but as far as I know, yes. It is true. A rise in blood pressure can cause a rupture, but cleaning out a stall…that's doubtful."

"But what if he was really angry? That could do it. He could have been furious with me, and then…" He stopped, unable to articulate this worst-case scenario.

Hope reached for his hands. "Look at me, Lucas. Your *dat*

had many faults, mainly with his management of money, but anger wasn't one of them. He was even-tempered. I never saw him upset at any of you boys. He'd shrug things off, laugh and say something like 'boys will be boys.' You did not cause your father's brain aneurysm."

Lucas sank back into his chair, brushed at his eyes and mumbled, "Okay. All right. I thought… But okay."

"Which brings us to the final thing I'd like to talk about today." Micah focused on Amos and Hope. "Lucas tells me that you two plan to marry."

"Yes," Hope said at the same moment that Amos said, "When the time is right."

"Lucas thinks that there's a possibility you've been waiting on him to feel more comfortable with Amos around."

Amos took that one. "This is an important time in Lucas's life. We don't want to rush anything or do anything that would interrupt the healthy balance he seems to be finding. At the same time, we do want to marry. I want to marry. I want Hope and Lucas as well as both of his brothers to be in my home. I want us to be a family."

Instead of agreeing or disagreeing with anything Amos said, Micah turned to Lucas. "Want to tell them?"

Dread clawed at the back of Amos's throat.

Tell them what?

That he couldn't abide living with Amos?

That he considered it a betrayal of his father?

That he would run away again if they married?

But it was none of those things. It was not Amos's worst nightmare and biggest fear.

Lucas looked at him and said, "I was afraid I'd kill you too."

"Kill me…" Amos had no idea what that meant. Lucas might as well have spoken French.

"I thought what I'd done wrong had killed my *dat*, and I figured…" He swiped at his eyes. "I figured that eventually I'd do the same to you."

Hope managed to say, "You didn't kill your *dat*, Lucas."

"I know that now."

"Son, are you saying that you want us to marry?" Amos studied Lucas. "Have you been afraid you may ruin our relationship?"

"Yes. That's what I'm saying."

Hope leaned forward and looked at her son. "Amos and I love each other, Lucas. And we are willing to wait if it will help you, but our love for each other is permanent. And Amos is a healthy man."

"Very healthy," Amos added.

"In a few years, you will be gone," his mother continued. She waved toward the window. "Doing whatever work you choose, living close by or far away. We can't know those details now. After that, Isaac will find his own independent way. And John, well, I expect John will marry by spring."

"Everything's changing." Lucas's voice was a whisper.

"Life is full of changes, for sure and certain."

"But there are also things amid the change that stay the same," Amos said. "Our love for you is one of them."

The wedding took place three weeks later.

Epilogue

The wedding was held on Amos's farm. The September weather cooperated. Leaves colored bright red and gold and brown clung to the limbs of trees. The sky was blue and the weather warm enough that Hope only needed a sweater—something Bethany had knit. It was a slightly darker shade than the light coral color of her dress and accented it perfectly.

"I can tell you're *kapp* over aprons for my *dat*," Ada said.

"Head over heels," Sarah whispered.

"He's lucky to have you," Becca chimed in.

"We all are," Bethany added.

But it was Eunice who summed it up well. "You make him happy, Hope. And that makes us happy. Plus, we'll finally have another boy in this family."

"Our husbands are boys," Sarah pointed out. "Plus Abram, Daniel and Peter."

"*Ya*, but I mean someone Josh's age. Someone for him to pal around with when he's older. Who knows? Maybe they'll want to go into business with me." Eunice had shared the news that she was expecting the week before. She put one hand on her belly, and with the other she drew an imaginary sign from left to right. "'Yoder and Lambert—Small Engine Repair.'"

At which point Isaac dashed into the bedroom. "Ezekiel said—" He stopped and stared at Hope. "You're so pretty!"

"*Danki*, son."

Isaac grinned. "Ezekiel said they're ready when you are."

They didn't walk downstairs right away. Instead they stood at the bedroom window, looking down on the array of chairs holding family, friends and coworkers. Hope was overcome with such happiness that she had to press her palm to her heart and pull in a slow, deep breath. She turned and studied Sarah, Becca, Eunice, Bethany and Ada. "I love you all," she said.

They responded with warm embraces and echoes of "We love you as well."

The guests were assembled. Ezekiel spent a few minutes alone with Hope and Amos, reminding them of their commitment to one another, which was reflective of Christ's commitment to the church. The ceremony that followed was simple and short.

When Ezekiel presented them to the guests, he said, "Everyone assembled here today, your children, grandchildren, friends and family in Christ, and I, as your bishop, wish you the blessing and mercy of God."

Hope met Amos's gaze, and she saw so much love and promise in his eyes that her knees felt weak. What had she done to deserve this man? What had she done to deserve this second family? Nothing, of course. *Gotte* was good. There had been a plan for her life all along. She just hadn't been able to see it.

She saw it now.

And she couldn't wait to get started building the life they would share together.

Amos had joyfully hosted five weddings for his five *doschdern* in the last few years. Never, during any of those precious events, had he thought that he would one day be the person standing beside the bishop, promising his love to another.

Sometimes *Gotte*'s plan for your life was so far beyond what you could imagine that it boggled the mind.

Hope gazed up at him, a tender smile on her face and tears shining in her eyes. What an amazing thing it was that after all they'd been through—both before Hope had moved to Shipshewana and after they'd met—their separate paths had become one.

With their families.

With their friends.

"Go forth in the Lord's name," Ezekiel said with a smile. "You are now man and wife."

There was whooping from some of the teens who worked for Amos. His own children cheered and pushed forward to be the first to congratulate them.

"I'm so happy for you both," Sarah said.

Sarah—his eldest. The *doschder* he had worried might have given up her chance at love so that she could take care of their family. Now she stood in front of him, Noah at her side and baby Grace in her arms.

Becca pulled them both into a tight hug that included her husband, Aaron, and their son, Daniel. "*Gotte* has great plans for you two," she said.

Hope winked at Amos as she said, "Who knows? We may even go on a mission trip."

Eunice looked radiant. Her pregnancy, though barely visible, was progressing smoothly. They would be welcoming a *boppli* after the first of the year. "I'm so happy for you. And for us." Zeb seconded that, and Josh held his hand up for high-fives from both Amos and Hope.

Bethany was next. "You made me cry," she confessed. "You both did."

"But it was a *gut* kind of cry?" Amos understood that

Bethany's feelings were often near the surface. It was one of the things that made her so dear to all of them.

"*Ya*, Dat. The best kind." Bethany threw her arms around them as Lydia attempted to squeeze in. Aaron held Daniel, who kept trying to swipe his *dat*'s hat off his head.

And then there was Ada. "I can tell you two love each other to the market and back."

"To the moon and back?" Hope asked, as she pulled Ada close.

"I haven't been to the moon, but the market is a *gut* long walk if your buggy breaks down." Ada stood in the circle of Hope's arm and reached for her *dat*, pulling him close. "Your love for my *dat* and his love for you will last a *gut* long time."

Ethan was holding their son, Peter, who attempted to launch himself into Ada's arms. "Come here, you little monkey."

Which left John, Lucas and Isaac.

They'd held back, allowed Amos's girls to greet them first. Now they looked almost shyly at their *mamm* and Amos.

"Congratulations," John said.

"Never had sisters before." Lucas blushed when Ada pulled him into a hug, but he didn't pull away.

Isaac bounced from foot to foot, hugged his mother, threw his arms around Amos, then said, "Christmas is going to be something else in this family," which caused everyone to laugh.

Amos realized he was right—Christmas, births, celebrations and possibly three more weddings. He looked at his beautiful bride, saw the tears shining in her eyes, and knew that she was thinking the same thing. He pulled her close and whispered, "They'll grow up fast, for sure and certain. But not today."

"Not today," she agreed.

"We'll always be there for each other."

"We will." She swiped at the tears slipping down her cheeks.

"Are you happy?"

"I am very happy."

"Want some lunch?" he asked mischievously.

"I'm starved."

"I've heard the bride and groom have a special place at the table.

"And I heard there's cake."

They stood there a little while longer, on a fine fall day, on the land he had come to love, amid a congregation that had become like a family. As their sons and *doschdern* fanned out among the guests, Amos understood that this was a special, happy moment he would always treasure. He also understood that he couldn't wait to begin the day-to-day of going about their lives together as one large, supportive, growing, energetic family.

"*Gotte* is good," Amos said.

To which Hope responded in the only way that made sense. "All the time."

They turned to make their way to the luncheon tables set up between the barn and the house. This farm had been a good home to him and to his girls. He hoped, he prayed, it would be as good a place to his new sons and all his and Hope's grandchildren.

His life had been calm for many years as he raised his girls. What had, for so many years, been a family of five was now a big, messy, growing, beautiful group of people who loved, cared for and supported one another.

Amos had much to be grateful for—the people in his life as well as the time he'd been given. He didn't plan to waste a minute of it.

* * * * *

Dear Reader,

Sometimes we get a second chance.

Hope Lambright has moved to Shipshewana for that very thing—a second chance to make a safe and happy home for her three sons. Hope is a hard worker, an optimist, and a believer that God is her refuge and provider...but she never dares to dream that this move might also bring her lasting happiness.

Amos Yoder has seen each of his five girls happily married. He can finally rest! Only now that his golden years are upon him, he's not sure what to do with himself. Then Hope moves to town, and everything Amos thought he knew about his dreams, his hopes, even himself fades away. *An Amish Widow's New Love* is the story of embracing the present, finding our next path, and daring to love again.

I hope you enjoyed reading this book. I welcome comments and letters at vannettachapman@gmail.com.

May we continue "giving thanks always for all things unto God the Father in the name of our Lord Jesus Christ" (Ephesians 5:20).

Blessings,
Vannetta

Harlequin® Reader Service

Enjoyed your book?

Try the perfect subscription for Romance readers and get more great books like this delivered right to your door.

See why over 10+ million readers have tried Harlequin Reader Service.

Start with a Free Welcome Collection with free books and a gift—valued over $20.

Choose any series in print or ebook. See website for details and order today:

TryReaderService.com/subscriptions

RSBPA2409